HOCUS POCUS
HOTEL

Hocus Pocus Hotel is published by Capstone
1710 Roe Crest Drive
North Mankato, Minnesota 56003
www.capstoneyoungreaders.com

Cataloging-in-Publication Data is available at the Library
of Congress website.

ISBN: 978-1-4342-6509-8 (paper-over-board)

Summary: Abracadabra, the founder of the Hocus Pocus
Hotel, has vanished! Charlie Hitchcock and Tyler Yu
team up again to solve this mystery and find their friend.
Then Tyler vanishes. But Charlie has reason to believe
that a mysterious thirteenth floor exists in the old hotel
. . .

This book is also available in two library-bound editions:
The Wizard and the Wormhole 978-1-4342-6507-4
The Prisoners of the Thirteenth Floor 978-1-4342-6508-1

Designer: Kristi Carlson
Photo credits: Shutterstock
Abracadabra Hotel illustration: Brann Garvey

Printed in China.
092013
007733LEOS14

The Thirteenth Mystery

BOOK 3

by Michael Dahl

illustrated by Lisa K. Weber

capstone

3 THE ABRACADABRA HOTEL

Table of

Contents

Impossible

From his desk near the back of Ms. Gimli's classroom, Charlie Hitchcock stared at the three impossible words.

ABRACADABRA IS MISSING.

Abracadabra, master of the impossible, the world's oldest living magician, missing? The same man who had made other people disappear, along with rabbits, airplanes, school buses, and the occasional elephant. How could he vanish?

If Abracadabra had disappeared on purpose, he would have let Charlie in on his plans. After all, the great performer — known as Brack to his friends — certainly thought of Charlie as a pal.

No way. Brack would have told me! Charlie thought. He scrunched up the note. *Or he would have told Ty, and Ty would have told me.*

Tyler Yu lived and worked at the world-famous Abracadabra Hotel. And while Charlie didn't exactly consider Ty his friend, the two boys had often worked together to solve puzzles surrounding the hotel's mysterious guests. It was Ty who had secretly handed the note to Charlie out in the hall, between classes. Charlie knew better than to say or ask anything at the time. Ty couldn't afford to let anyone know that he was on speaking terms with Charlie Hitchcock, the smartest kid in Blackstone Middle School, and therefore the school's biggest nerd.

If Brack didn't say anything to me or Ty, thought Charlie, *then his disappearance wasn't planned. An accident?*

Charlie heard an odd *tap-tap* sound.

"What's that tapping?" asked Ms. Gimli from the front of the classroom.

Scotter Larson raised his hand. "I believe," he began without being called on, "it's Morse Code, Ms. Gimli."

"Morse Code?" Ms. Gimli repeated. "Well, whoever is doing it should stop."

"It's not me, Ms. Gimli," said Scotter. The blond boy sat up straighter in his desk. "Even though I was the youngest Scout in the tri-state area to receive a badge for Morse Code."

Something hit Charlie on the shoulder. He looked up and saw Tyler Yu standing just outside the door of Ms. Gimli's room.

The tall boy looked angry. He always looked angry. He tapped harder against the doorframe with a pen.

"Impossible," said Scotter Larson. "It doesn't make sense."

Ms. Gimli turned from the whiteboard and looked at Scotter. "What is impossible?"

"The Morse Code message," Scotter said. "The Morse message says H-V-R-R-Y-V-P. But that's not a word."

Charlie wrote down the letters in his notebook.

H.V.R.R.Y.V.P.

Scotter may think it's not a word, he thought, *but it is. Two words, actually.*

Charlie knew that in order to solve a puzzle you sometimes needed to take into account unpredictable factors. And the most unpredictable factors were personalities.

In this case, the personality of the person actually sending the Morse Code message: Tyler Wu. Ty knew a lot about secrets and strategy. But he wasn't the best speller.

Tyler's making a mistake, thought Charlie. *He's*

using three dots instead of two to spell a Morse letter. He doesn't mean V, he means U. He's telling me to hurry up!

Charlie looked at Tyler. The tall boy's face was turning red. His eyes were glowing.

Charlie rushed up to Ms. Gimli. "Uh, may I go to the lavatory?" he whispered.

"Can't you wait until lunch?"

"I don't think so."

"Then hurry up," said the teacher.

"Hurry up?" said Scotter to himself.

He's figuring it out, thought Charlie. He gathered up his things and left the room.

"What took you so long?" Ty spat out. "You saw the note!" He turned and headed down the hall. "And before you say anything, yeah, I know the Morse Code was spelled wrong. I did that on purpose so no one else would figure it out."

"Wait!" said Charlie, running alongside. "Where are you going?"

Tyler stopped. He fixed Charlie with a steely

look, as if he were pinning the boy to the wall. "I thought you figured that out, too. Aren't you the smartest kid in school?"

Charlie said, "You're going to the hotel? Now? In the middle of the day?"

Tyler smiled, but it was a cold smile. "Wrong, Brainiac. *We're* going to the hotel. Now. In the middle of the day. Our friend needs us."

And that was all Charlie needed to hear.

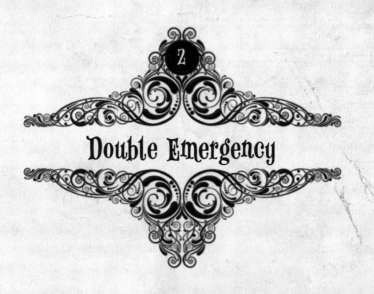

Double Emergency

It was raining by the time Charlie and Ty reached the Abracadabra Hotel in an old section of downtown Blackstone.

The ancient building—known to its residents as the Hocus Pocus Hotel, but officially named for its founder, Abracadabra — raised its towers toward the dark churning clouds.

When the boys walked through the glass double doors, they passed from rain, gloom, and thunder to bright lights, laughter, and excited voices. The vast lobby was completely stuffed with people.

"What's going on?" asked Charlie. "Is it a party?"

"Tyler!" yelled a voice. The boys saw a young girl elbowing her way through the crowd. It was Annie Solo, who worked at the front desk.

"Tyler," she repeated, trying to catch her breath. "I'm so glad to see you. You got my text!"

"Text?" Ty said, frowning. "Uh, nope. No text. I don't have a phone. You must have had the wrong number or something."

"I beeped you, too," Annie said. "Twice. Maybe three times."

"Annie, you know I can't have my beeper on at school," Tyler said.

Charlie guessed that Tyler had probably been ignoring the girl's messages.

Annie made it no secret that she had a crush on Tyler. Ty, however, felt differently.

He grabbed Charlie by the collar and started using him as a human plow to push through the crowd. "Sorry, but I'm in the middle of an emergency here," said Ty.

"I'll say," said Annie, following closely. "This afternoon's the Friday special preview, as you know. And the tech guy never showed up for it, and I knew that you've worked the light booth before, so —"

"Wait a minute. What are you talking about, Annie?" asked Charlie. It was hard for him to hear her while being shoved between men wearing suits and women in long gowns that glittered like plastic wrap.

"The magic show preview," Annie explained. "The preview of David Dragonstone before tonight's big show! He goes on in half an hour, but we don't have anyone to run the lights for the stage."

"Annie," said Tyler, without stopping or looking back, "I can't right now."

"But you're not in school," Annie pointed out.

"Neither are you," Tyler shot back.

"I'm in a work program, remember?" said Annie. "Every Wednesday and Friday afternoon. What's your excuse?"

"Emergency," said Tyler. "Besides, you wanted me to come."

"Because your mother asked me to," Annie said. "And if she finds out you left school, but not to help me, then . . ."

Tyler's mother, Miranda Yu, was the hotel manager for the Abracadabra. His dad, Walter Yu, was the head chef of the hotel restaurant, the Top Hat. Although Charlie had met them only briefly, he knew they were deadly serious about work. He often wondered if any one of the Yus ever smiled.

Tyler stopped.

The three of them had squeezed a path through the crowd and stood near the row of elevators. Ty's shoulders slumped, and he looked down at his boots.

"Okay, fine," he said. "I'll run the lights for the afternoon show. But I better get paid for it." He turned to Charlie. "You go up to Brack's place and search for clues. Find out where he went in the hotel."

"You said he was missing," said Charlie.

"Yeah, but he never left the hotel," Ty told him.

"How do you know that?" Charlie asked.

"Surveillance cameras," said Tyler.

"So that's what you were looking at in the office last night," said Annie.

Tyler ignored her. "There are cameras all over the lobby," he told Charlie. "See?" Charlie followed Ty's pointed finger and noticed small gold-colored gadgets attached to the lobby's pillars.

"We can see anyone going out or coming in through the hotel doors," said Ty. "There are more cameras at the loading dock in the alley. But Brack wasn't on any of them. He has to be somewhere in the building."

Unless he found a magic way out, thought Charlie.

"Brack was supposed to be at Dragonstone's rehearsal last night, but he never showed up," chimed in Annie.

"I know," said Ty. "That's why I'm worried. He's been gone for, like, at least eighteen hours now."

Charlie knew Brack would never miss a rehearsal. He was way too good a performer for that.

Was he hurt? Or sick? Brack was older than the hotel bearing his name, and old people sometimes had health problems.

"He's gone. Vanished," said Ty.

"Can the hotel's security cameras tell us

where Brack went inside the hotel?" asked Charlie. "It must be caught on film."

"They only look at the exits and entrances," said Ty. "Mom wants to upgrade for the whole hotel, but she hasn't been able to yet."

Annie grabbed Tyler's arm. "Okay. We need to hurry," she said. "They're opening the doors for the preview show in ten minutes."

"Go up to Brack's and look for clues," said Ty. "Then come back here and we'll search the hotel together."

"I'd love to!" said Annie.

Tyler opened his mouth to object, but Annie quickly led him away from the crowd and through another door.

"Don't worry," Charlie called out to Ty's vanishing back. "I'll be fine."

Charlie entered an elevator and pushed the gold button at the very top.

Don't worry? he asked himself. *Who am I*

*kidding? I skipped school, Brack is missing, and I don't
know what I'm supposed to look for.*

It was the perfect time to worry.

Clues on the Carpet

The spring shower had grown into a raging thunderstorm. Wind and rain whipped fiercely around the tall downtown buildings as Charlie ran from the shelter of the elevator toward Brack's home. The magician's house was perched on the rooftop of the old hotel. It was surrounded by empty flower gardens and leafless trees that stuck out of cement pots like upside-down claws scratching the air.

When Charlie reached the front door and grasped the knob, he was cold and soaked with rain.

I'm so stupid, thought Charlie. *I should have asked Annie for a key to get into Brack's place. Now what am I going to do?*

Charlie shivered and tried the knob. The door was unlocked. Cautiously, he stepped inside. The hall light was on. "Brack!" he called.

As he stepped forward, rain puddled on the carpet around his shoes. Charlie dropped his backpack on the floor and yelled again. "Brack!"

There was no answer.

Charlie felt odd looking through his friend's house while he was gone. As if he were breaking the law. But he knew he had to do it. He had to search for clues.

Like the empty cup on the table in a small sitting room. That was the only other room in

Brack's apartment where the lights were on. The room was full of magical props from hundreds of stage shows. The walls were covered with colorful, old-fashioned posters. But the empty cup seemed out of place to Charlie.

He picked it up and sniffed. Yuck! Coffee. He hated the taste and smell of coffee. Come to think of it, so did Brack. So why was it there? For a guest?

Why are the lights on? he wondered. *Annie said Brack never showed up at the magic show rehearsal last night. Brack must have been here, and then disappeared before morning.*

Charlie noticed a table nearby that held leather-bound books and more magic props. In the middle of the table were two items that snagged his attention.

A cardboard tube lay on a yellow notepad. The tube was empty. A name was stamped at one end: LAND REGISTRAR, BLACKSTONE COUNTY.

On the yellow pad were a few words, scrawled in pencil.

Tiger lily here? Charlie stood back up and looked quickly around the room. There were no flowers in here. What did Brack mean?

And Charlie knew that the Hocus Pocus Hotel did not have a thirteenth floor. Not officially. It had a floor above the twelfth one, of course, but it wasn't numbered thirteen. It was called the fourteenth floor. Many hotels did the same trick. Lots of people were superstitious and refused to sleep on an unlucky thirteenth floor. So hotels just dropped the 13 and substituted 14 in its place.

Maybe Brack was writing about a magic trick for one of his shows.

Lightning flashed through the windows of the house.

I better get back downstairs, thought Charlie. He tore the paper off the pad and stuffed it into his backpack.

He made one last quick tour of the house to make sure the windows and other doors were locked. There was no way in or out except through the front door. Charlie stood, his hand on the doorknob, looking out at the fierce storm.

Brack must have been in a hurry when he left, Charlie thought. *Otherwise he would have locked the door. Or maybe he realized he was hurrying to the rehearsal, and he just forgot.*

Charlie frowned.

Nothing in Brack's house seemed to be a real clue. The magician might have been visiting with an old friend who liked coffee. Maybe he'd been working on a new magic trick that involved carpets and flowers, and then headed down to the rehearsal. Nothing unusual.

Charlie picked up his backpack and froze.

On the damp carpet, lay an object he had not seen before. It had been hidden by his pack. He squatted down and picked it up. A clump of hair.

Fake red hair.

4

The Dragonstone Disappearance

"Find anything?" asked Ty when Charlie got back downstairs.

Charlie nodded. "Yeah," he said, reaching into his backpack. "Wait till you see —"

"Tyler!" yelled Annie. "It's about to start."

The three of them were standing inside the booth that controlled the lighting for the Abracadabra Theatre.

The booth was on the rear wall of the theater, opposite the stage, and high above the audience. Charlie could see the tops of five hundred heads, facing the stage and waiting for the entrance of David Dragonstone.

"Here goes," said Ty, sliding a lever on the huge control panel.

Bright lights lit up the stage and a roar of applause shook the walls. David Dragonstone — tall, thin, with piercing eyes — walked out onto the stage and waved.

"That guy's the magician?" said Ty. "He looks like a kid."

He has red hair, thought Charlie.

The boys and Annie watched the entire show, which lasted an hour. Tyler kept busy reading the light cues from sheets on a clipboard.

Then came the final trick of the performance.

On the stage far below, bathed in brilliant light, several assistants strapped Dragonstone into a straitjacket. A chain was wrapped around his ankles. Then a hook was attached to the chain and the young, redheaded magician was hoisted into the air.

The audience gasped. Dragonstone rose higher and higher. He came to rest, thirty feet above the stage, upside down. Then, without warning, a strange man climbed onto the stage.

The stranger wore a flowing black robe. He had dark hair that hung to his shoulders and a black mustache and pointed beard. "Ladies and gentlemen," said the man in a commanding voice. "Behold, the amazing Dragonstone, in his final act of the evening."

He gestured to the young magician twisting high above him. "Dragonstone has amazed audiences throughout the world. It is my humble duty and great pleasure, as the Wizard DeVille, to announce this final feat of illusion and leger-demain."

"Leger what?" asked Ty.

"It means trickery," said Annie. "Like a trick that a magician can do with his hands."

Dragonstone can't use his hands, strapped in that jacket, thought Charlie. *There's no way out of it.*

"Behold!" cried the wizard. "And tremble with fear!"

The hook holding David Dragonstone snapped open. The magician plunged headfirst, still straitjacketed, toward the stage, thirty feet below.

The straitjacket hit the stage. But instead of a thud, it made hardly a sound.

The wizard, DeVille, ran over to the lifeless form. He lifted it up easily with one hand. It was only the straitjacket, and it was empty. Dragonstone had fallen toward the stage, but he never reached it.

The redheaded magician had completely disappeared.

"Dragonstone has disappeared," shouted DeVille.

A member of the audience began clapping. Then another. And another. Soon everyone in the audience was cheering and shouting.

"What a trick!" said Annie.

"But who is that guy?" said Ty.

The magician named DeVille bugged Charlie, too. Something was not right. Now two magicians were missing.

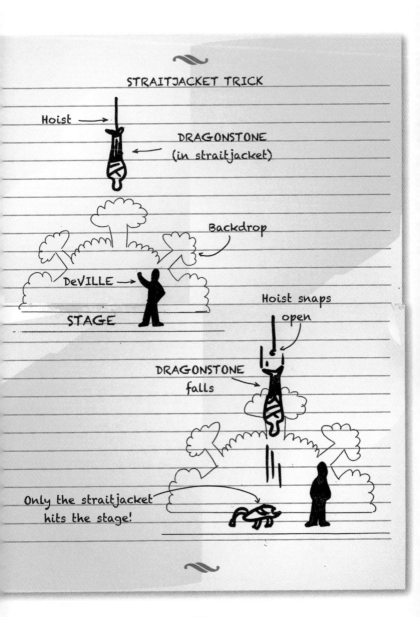

5

The Glass Keyhole

DeVille, his eyes flashing above his dark mustache, raised his gloved hands to the audience.

"Ladies and gentlemen," he said, "you have witnessed the power of Monsieur Dragonstone to disappear in midair. But where, I ask you, has he gone?"

The audience grew still. People who were standing sat back down.

"This is but the first half of the finale," said DeVille. "I now need a volunteer from the audience."

A young man stood up near the front of the stage.

"I know that guy," said Tyler, peering out the light booth window.

"That's Joey Bingham," said Charlie. "The news reporter. What's he up to?"

DeVille motioned for the reporter to join him onstage. "This young man shall be my witness," said DeVille. "And he will be your eyes." DeVille waved his hands again and a large screen was lowered onto the stage.

"Tyler!" yelled Annie. "The projector button."

"Oh yeah, right," said Ty. He quickly scanned the control panel and pressed a button. A flash of blue light hit the screen.

DeVille presented a small object to Joey

Bingham. "Take this camera, young man," said the wizard. "And follow me." He turned to the audience. "Now, you shall see the amazing Dragonstone reappear, in a completely different part of the hotel. Watch the screen."

Charlie and the others saw shapes and movement on the stage screen. They saw DeVille as he walked off the stage and through a door, into a hallway, and then through the hotel lobby. DeVille stopped at the elevators and faced Joey's camera. "We shall now go up to the twelfth floor," said DeVille. "There, we will witness an even more incredible illusion."

Charlie turned to Ty, who was staring intently at the screen. "I'm going up there," Charlie said.

"Me too," said Tyler.

"But what about the booth?" said Annie.

"Nothing to it," said Ty. "Light on, lights off. Besides, the projector button will stay on through the rest of the trick."

"But what if —"

"I've got to make sure Hitchcock doesn't get into any trouble," said Ty. "He's too puny to take care of himself." The two boys rushed out of the light booth and reached the lobby elevators.

DeVille and Joey were already gone.

"Puny, huh?" asked Charlie.

"Get in the elevator," said Ty.

Ping! When the elevator doors slid open on the twelfth floor, the boys slipped out.

"Down there," said Tyler.

At the end of the hall, DeVille and Joey were turning a corner.

The boys rushed up to join them. Joey, hearing their footsteps, turned around, his camera facing them.

Great, thought Charlie. *Now the whole audience can see us.*

DeVille stopped when he saw the newcomers. He drew up his shoulders and addressed the camera, with great dignity. "Excellent. We have been joined by two new witnesses. Complete strangers, I assure you. They shall convince you, ladies and gentlemen of the audience, that what they see, what you see from your seats, is absolutely real!"

After a few more turns through the maze-like hallways, DeVille came to a sudden stop. "This is it," he said, and gestured to Joey. "Take a picture of that doorway."

"What the heck is that?" asked Joey.

"Have you seen that before?" Charlie whispered to Ty.

The taller boy nodded. "I avoid it when I come up here," he said. "There's no way to get through it."

The door was something that could only be seen in a hotel built by magicians.

It was made of glass and led into another dim hallway that could be clearly seen on the other side. But no one could enter the hallway, because the door was really much more of a window than a door.

It did not open. There were no hinges. In the exact center of the glass door was a small opening shaped like a keyhole.

DeVille's gleaming eyes shot at Tyler. "Since you work here, young man, then you must know that there is no way through this glass door."

Joey swung the camera up at the tall boy.

"Yeah, that's right," answered Ty. "It's just for fun. This is a trick door made by Abracadabra when he built the hotel. It's just sort of, like, a joke."

"Or perhaps a challenge to other magicians," said DeVille. "And what is at the end of this hallway on the other side of the glass?"

"It connects to the other hallways," said Ty. "But you have to walk all the way around to reach it."

DeVille nodded. "Would you be so kind as to stand at the other end of that hallway?" he said. "You shall be our guard. Make sure no one gets in or out of the hallway."

Tyler looked at Charlie and shrugged. "Okay, fine," he said. Then he took off.

DeVille spoke to the camera.

"There is no one up here except myself and these three witnesses, ladies and gentlemen," he said. "I checked with the hotel staff, and no one is in any of the rooms on this floor. All the doors are locked. But —" He pulled a long, yellow ribbon from his coat. Then he added, "Someone invisible is with us. The spirit of Dragonstone. He is in that mysterious hallway. Unable to reach us through the solid glass door. But, by using this ribbon which I obtained while on a journey, from my brother wizards in Katmandu, I shall open a mystic wormhole and rescue the invisible Dragonstone."

DeVille rolled up a piece of the ribbon and then stuffed it through the tiny keyhole, where it cascaded in a long strand down the other side.

"I shall hold this end," said the magician, keeping a firm hold on the ribbon.

Next, DeVille rolled a metal frame in front of the glass door. The magician pulled down black curtains on the frame, effectively screening the glass door from the viewers' eyes. The ribbon passed through the curtains. DeVille stood just outside the frame, where Joey's camera could still see him, one end of the ribbon still in his hand.

"Watch the ribbon," said DeVille. "I shall pull it back through the keyhole and onto this side of the solid glass door."

Slowly, ever so slowly, the dark haired magician pulled the yellow ribbon through the black curtains. It kept coming.

What's the big deal? thought Charlie. *He's just pulling the ribbon back through the keyhole. Why won't he let us watch it happen?*

"Hey!" shouted Joey. The ribbon stopped. DeVille held it in both hands now, and Charlie could see that the ribbon wasn't coming any farther. It must have caught on something.

"Is it stuck?" Joey asked, walking closer to the ribbon.

"How could it be stuck?" asked DeVille. "The keyhole is smooth, and there is nothing between it and the curtains. Perhaps it has found something in the wormhole."

Charlie felt a growing coldness along his spine.

"Mr. Hitchcock," said DeVille. "Would you be so kind as to pull the curtains open for our audience?"

Charlie walked over, grabbed a curtain., and yanked it aside.

Joey almost dropped his camera.

In front of them, on the same side of the glass door as them and DeVille, stood the redheaded Dragonstone, with the yellow silk ribbon tied around his waist.

David Dragonstone bowed to the camera. "Thank you, Monsieur DeVille," he said, smiling, "for rescuing me from the Beyond. And thank you, everyone, for coming to this afternoon's premiere."

DeVille reached over and snapped off the camera.

"Magnificent," said DeVille, clapping the other magician on the back.

"What's going on?" came a voice.

Tyler ran up to the glass door from the other side. His eyes grew wide as he saw Dragonstone. "Hey, how did he get over there?"

"Through a wormhole," said Joey.

Charlie noticed a worried look on the redheaded man's face. But DeVille gave him a reassuring look.

"Don't worry," said DeVille. "That young man in the elegant T-shirt and jeans is another volunteer. He was making sure no one could enter from the far end."

"Ah, thank you for your assistance," Dragonstone said to Tyler. Turning to DeVille, he added, "We should return to the stage."

"But how did you get here?" asked Joey. "You weren't inside that flimsy frame. You couldn't hide inside a curtain."

"There was no one in the hallway when I got to the other side," said Tyler.

"Wizardry," said DeVille with a wave of his hand.

The magicians walked off, followed by a chattering Joey, trying to get a scoop for his paper.

"I can see the headline now," said Joey. "The Hair-Raising Houdini of the Hocus Pocus Hotel!"

"Young man!" came the dwindling voice of the retreating wizard. "It's the Abracadabra, if you don't mind."

Tyler and Charlie stared at one another through the solid glass door.

"How'd he do it, Hitch?" asked Tyler.

Both boys felt the smooth glass. It was solid. And the keyhole was clearly too small for anyone to pass through.

"You didn't see anything over there?" asked Charlie.

"Nothing," said Ty. "And that hall is long. I could barely see the black curtain come down over the door. But I did hear a funny noise."

"Funny?"

"Like a thump. Or someone jumping."

Tyler shook his head as if to clear it. "I'm just glad this stupid show is over. Meet me at the elevators and we'll head up to Brack's."

Charlie ran back to the elevators. On the way he glanced at the wallpaper in the hall. It was covered with prints of fancy-looking flowers. Tiger lilies? No, they looked more like roses.

The hall with the elevators was quiet. The two magicians and Joey must have already gone back to the theater.

As Charlie stood and waited for Ty, he thought back to the amazing illusion he had just witnessed. How did Dragonstone appear? Had he been hiding somewhere in that hallway? Even if he was, how did he pass through the solid glass

door? No one could have hidden in that frame or curtains. Dragonstone must have come from the other side of the glass. But how?

And what was taking Tyler so long?

"Ty," shouted Charlie. No answer. Charlie listened but didn't hear any approaching footsteps. "Ty!" he called again.

Charlie ran down several halls, hoping he was going in the direction of the blocked hallway.

He could just make out the curtains that had been left on the other side of the glass door. This was the place. So where was Tyler? They should have run into each other.

Charlie called a few more times, but heard nothing. He started to sweat. Something was wrong. He ran back to the elevators. Still no Ty.

He waited a few more minutes. He shouted one last time. Then he got on an elevator and descended to the main floor, alone.

6

Beard and Mustache

Charlie pushed through crowds of people streaming through the lobby as they exited the theater. They were heading toward the front doors, where they opened umbrellas to face the pouring rain, or waved their arms for honking taxicabs.

When Charlie reached the front desk he was

disappointed not to see Tyler. He was surprised to see Annie, though. Her familiar smile was twisted into a frown.

"Where have you been?" she said. "Where's Tyler?"

"I don't know," said Charlie. "I thought he was down here."

"Well, he's not!" she said. "And I had to figure out those lights all by myself. The audience was in the dark for ten minutes!"

"He told me to meet him at the elevators, but he never showed up," said Charlie.

Wait a minute. Tyler said something else before I left him, thought Charlie. *Something that didn't make sense at the time.*

"Typical," said Annie, folding her arms. She looked back at the front desk, where another young woman with thick dark hair was frantically helping five customers at the same time. Annie sighed. "I guess I have to get to work," she said.

"Wait," said Charlie. "I think Tyler disappeared."

"Of course he did," said Annie, walking away.

"I mean — disappeared!"

Annie stopped in midstride. She turned to look at Charlie. "You mean disappeared like Brack?"

"I'm worried," said Charlie. "After everything happened, Ty and I were supposed to meet back at the elevators. Like I said, he never showed up. Then I ran around all the halls but didn't see him."

"I hope he's not hurt," Annie said.

"Was DeVille right?" asked Charlie. "There's no one on that floor?"

Annie nodded. "And all the doors are locked." She shook her head. "Poor, poor Tyler."

"Annie!" The girl at the desk looked upset.

"I'll be right there, Cozette," called Annie.

"But we need to find Ty," said Charlie. "And Brack."

Annie stepped toward Charlie and grabbed his hand. Suddenly, she looked very serious. Annie spoke in a low tone. Her lips moved close to his ear. She whispered, "Meet me on the twelfth floor in ten minutes. We'll look for them together." Then she stood up and hurried back to the desk.

As she walked away, Charlie noticed that he was holding something in his hand. *She was just giving me a key.* It was a passkey to all the rooms in the hotel.

Instead of going to the twelfth floor, Charlie headed backstage. He remembered the hunk of red hair from Brack's carpet. He was sure it had something to do with the redheaded David Dragonstone.

In the theater, men and women were moving props, sweeping the stage, and guiding racks of costumes through the workspace. All the lights were on.

"Excuse me," said Charlie to a woman walking

past with a case full of snakes. "Can you tell me where the magicians are?"

The woman used the case to point. "The dressing room's over that way," she said.

"Thanks," Charlie said. "Hey, are those snakes real?"

"Maybe," the woman said, smiling.

Charlie rushed over to the dressing room. It was locked. He put his ear to the door and heard nothing inside. Making sure no one was watching him, he used the passkey and let himself in. Then he groped for a light switch near the door.

When the lights came on, Charlie found himself in a long narrow room with a row of mirrors along one wall. In front of the mirrors ran a low counter and several chairs. Plastic containers sat on the counter. Opening them, Charlie saw pencils, brushes, sponges, and tubes of different colors of makeup.

Turbans and top hats hung from hooks on

the walls, along with capes, several straitjackets, and an undersea diver's outfit. Closets stood at each end of the room. Charlie searched through those as well. He wasn't exactly sure what he was looking for, but he knew he had to start somewhere.

I found the red hair when I wasn't expecting it, he thought, *so if I just keep looking, maybe —*

Then he saw it, hanging on a hook at the back of one of the closets. A fake beard and mustache, both made of red hair. A section of hair on one side of the beard was missing. Charlie pulled the red hair from his pocket and held it up to the beard.

A perfect match.

So Dragonstone had been upstairs talking to Brack. But how did the hair end up on the floor? Did Brack pull it off the man's face? Was there a struggle?

Charlie grew more worried about the missing magician. And Ty.

I've got to find them, he thought.

Charlie stuffed the beard into his backpack. He was backing out of the closet, when he heard a noise. Someone was unlocking the door.

He pushed through the costumes toward the back of the closet. He flattened against the wall and slid behind a dark furry robe that looked like a bearskin. Something scraped at his side, and he almost gasped.

In the dim light that filtered into the closet from the dressing room, he saw what had made the scraping sound. A rolled-up piece of blue paper leaned against the wall. On the upper edge he saw an official looking stamp. LAND REGISTRAR, BLACKSTONE COUNTY

Like the one in Brack's house, thought Charlie. It was too much of a coincidence that the young magician's closet held two items from the home of the missing Abracadabra. As quietly and quickly as he could, Charlie slipped the paper roll inside his backpack.

The door to the dressing room was opening. Charlie heard footsteps. A small thud. Someone breathing. Then everything went black. The lights had snapped off. Slowly, the door squeaked shut and he heard the lock click.

Charlie hated the dark. It was the one thing that truly frightened him. He wasn't bothered by heights, spiders, snakes, or even tight spaces. In the light, at least, you could see those things. But in the dark, you were never sure what was there.

Was someone still in the room with him?

Charlie held his breath. Then he counted to a hundred. When he still heard nothing from the dressing room, he silently shuffled out of the closet. Moving through the hanging clothes in the darkness felt like walking through a crowd of people. Or through thick black curtains.

Black curtains!

That's what Ty had said upstairs. Something about DeVille's curtains that didn't sound quite right.

Charlie slid his hands gently along the wall. He felt the doorframe and then the knob.

He turned the knob, and then pulled the door open. The lights from the stage were almost blinding.

Then he saw, on the counter by the mirror, a huge vase that hadn't been there before. It held a dozen roses and a small card. He reached over and read the card.

CONGRATULATIONS
ON YOUR PREVIEW!
MAGNIFIQUE!
Th___DeV.

Charlie sighed, relieved. The unseen footsteps hadn't been looking for him. They had simply dropped off the flowers.

But what an odd way to sign your name. "The DeV."?

Charlie replaced the card, closed the door, and then hurried back to the elevators to show Annie what he had found.

The Stairs Between

"When was Brack supposed to meet Dragonstone last night?" asked Charlie.

"The rehearsal was at eight o'clock," answered Annie. "When Brack never showed up, we called upstairs, but he didn't answer."

They were standing in a hallway on the twelfth floor. They figured that floor was the best place to start their search for Ty. And if they found Ty, they might find Brack.

Charlie figured it was too much of a coincidence that both friends had vanished within 24 hours of each other. Their disappearances had to be connected.

"And Dragonstone was there already?" said Charlie.

Annie nodded. "He got to the hotel right before the rehearsal. He didn't even have time to eat or go to his room. And while we waited onstage, he said that he wanted Brack to introduce his final act, the Empty Straitjacket."

"Really?" said Charlie. "So who was that DeVille guy?"

"A friend of Mr. Dragonstone's," said Annie. "When the rehearsal was almost over and Brack still hadn't shown up, Dragonstone called DeVille. DeVille came to the hotel this morning."

"This morning?"

"Yes, right after Tyler left for school."

"So when did they have time to rehearse the Glass Door Trick?" asked Charlie.

"I'm not sure about that," said Annie. "I don't think Dragonstone even mentioned it last night. It seemed like something DeVille came up with on his own."

There's something fishy about that, thought Charlie. But if Brack disappeared last night, Dragonstone might not be involved. Not if he was at rehearsal the whole time Brack was absent.

Still, magicians were awfully tricky characters.

"Now what was it you wanted to show me?" asked Annie, sidling up closer to him.

Charlie pulled out the fake red beard and mustache from his backpack and explained them to her.

Then he knelt down on the thick hallway carpet and unrolled the blue paper he had found in the dressing room closet. Annie knelt down next to him.

"I found this in Dragonstone's dressing room," Charlie told her. "I'm sure it came out of an empty tube I found up at Brack's place. This stamp is on both of them." He pointed to the official words at the edge of the paper. He saw two more words he hadn't noticed before in the dim closet: ORIGINAL COPY.

Annie gasped. "It's the hotel," she said. "The Hocus Pocus — I mean, the Abracadabra. It's the whole hotel."

The blue roll of paper was actually made up of several sheets. And as Charlie stared at the top sheet in front of them, he realized Annie was right. These were blueprints for the old hotel.

It made sense that Brack would have kept them over the years, knowing how much the building meant to him.

"There's the theater," Annie said, pointing. "There's the lobby. Those circles are the pillars. There are the elevators."

Charlie flipped through the sheets. One of

them showed a plan of the roof. "That's Brack's place," he said.

"See if you can find the twelfth floor," said Annie. "See if it has the glass door and keyhole in it."

"Good idea," said Charlie. He separated all the sheets and laid them out next to each other. Soon the hallway seemed to be re-carpeted with blue paper.

"There must be a dozen pages," said Annie.

"One for each floor," said Charlie.

But though they carefully examined each sheet, they could not find one for Floor 12.

"Here's fourteen," said Annie. "Twelve is missing!"

"No, said Charlie. "It's been stolen. The twelfth floor is where the magic act took place, and the floor where Ty disappeared. Someone took that page on purpose."

"Mr. Dragonstone?" whispered Annie.

"Look at this," said Charlie.

He pulled a page from the far end of the sheets.

"It's the whole hotel," said Annie.

Charlie liked the drawing. Faint white lines against a blue background showed the entire building, floor by floor, room by room.

"Here's the glass door," Annie said. "See?"

"Aha!" Charlie said. "*That's* how it was done!"

A thump sounded somewhere in the hall. Annie and Charlie froze and stared at each other.

"What was that?" whispered Annie.

"Footsteps?" asked Charlie.

They both held their breath and listened. The thumping stopped.

"The only way to get to these floors is by elevator, right?" whispered Charlie.

"And the stairwells," said Annie. "Every hotel needs stairs in case there's a fire. Then the elevators shut off, and even if you're on the twentieth floor, you have to use the stairs."

"Where are they?" said Charlie.

After a few moments of scanning the sheets, they found the drawing of the stairwell on the west side of the building. Something looked odd.

"Why is that flight of stairs longer than the others?" Charlie asked.

Annie peered closer. "You're right. The stairs from twelve to fourteen are longer. Weird."

A light exploded in Charlie's brain. *That's it, that's it!* he thought.

"Are you going to be sick?" asked Annie.

"The stairs!" he shouted. "The stairs!"

They heard another thump. This one seemed closer.

Charlie jumped to his feet. "We don't have any time to lose. Come on, where's the door to the stairs?"

Annie's face was pale. "But Charlie, those noises . . ."

"If I'm right," said Charlie, "I think someone is trying to communicate with us."

"A ghost?" asked Annie.

"No," said Charlie with a smile. "Ty."

Taking Steps

Annie led Charlie down three hallways, up a short flight of steps, along another hall curved like a macaroni noodle, and at last to a metal door decorated with brass rabbits. The heavy door opened swithout a creak. Inside the echoing stairwell, the bannisters gleamed with dark wood. Charlie wished it were brighter in the stairwell. The small lamps shaped like tulips provided very little light.

"Up to the fourteenth floor," he said. "And count the steps."

They climbed to the next landing, turned, and climbed a second flight of stairs to reach a metal door with a brass "XIV" stamped at the top. "How many steps?" asked Charlie.

"Seventeen on each flight," said Annie. "So thirty-four steps between the twelfth floor and the fourteenth."

"Great," said Charlie. "Now we go up to the fifteenth."

Once they reached the fifteenth floor's landing, Annie looked amazed. "Only nine steps for each flight."

"That's eighteen in all," said Charlie. "So the space between twelve and fourteen is twice the height between the other floors."

Annie gasped. "Which means . . ."

Charlie smiled. "There's a thirteenth floor!"

Annie ran back down to the fourteenth floor, and then half a flight below that. Charlie followed her.

Annie searched the wall beneath the dim tulips. "I don't see any way in," she said.

"I don't think there's a door here," said Charlie. "I think the entrance is on the twelfth or fourteenth floor. My guess is that Dragonstone and DeVille have rooms on fourteen."

"Right," said Annie. "Two rooms next to each other."

"Let's go back to the hall on the twelfth floor. Where they did the magic trick," said Charlie. "I know how Dragonstone disappeared on stage, but it's —"

Annie stopped him. "You do?" she said.

"Simple mirrors," said Charlie. "And some legerdemain. But I'm still puzzled about the keyhole trick. How did Dragonstone appear behind that glass door in the first place? I think it has something to do with the thirteenth floor."

He was also sure that the mysterious, hidden floor had something to do with the disappearance of his two friends.

Annie and Charlie passed through the metal door carved with rabbits and ran along the curving hallway. Wind rattled the hall's windows. Lightning flashed. The storm was growing stronger.

Beep . . . beep . . .

Annie stopped and fished something out of her pocket. "No, it's my beeper. So Mrs. Yu can reach us wherever we are in the hotel. It's a big place, you know." Annie groaned. "It's a 999. That means an emergency."

Minutes later, the two were walking through the hotel lobby again. It seemed empty to Charlie, now that the crowds from the preview magic show were gone.

But when he and Annie walked around one of the tall marble pillars, Charlie stopped in his tracks. A familiar figure stood at the front desk, his face cruel and triumphant, his arms folded across his chest, as he spoke to Mr. and Mrs. Yu, Tyler's parents. "I shall be taking steps . . ." the figure was saying.

"Mr. Theopolis!" said Charlie.

The magician turned a sour face toward the boy. "Please, young man. The Great and Powerful Theopolis," he said. "And soon to be greater and more powerful."

Miranda Yu, in a sleek purple suit, looked unhappy. "I find this highly irregular, Mr. Theopolis," she said.

"It's completely regular, I assure you," Theopolis said. "And also legal."

Walter Yu took off his chef's hat and twisted it in his hands. Miranda Yu's face grew red. "You can't be serious," she said.

"Deadly serious," said Theopolis. "Which is why I checked everything with the Registrar's office before I came here."

Registrar! thought Charlie.

"If Brack does not make his special payment for the hotel's mortgage within the next twenty-four hours," said Theopolis with a toothy grin, "then the Abracadabra Hotel is mine!"

Deadline for Abracadabra

"What's going on?" cried Annie.

Mrs. Yu sighed. "It's not your problem, Annie," she said. "Don't worry about it."

Theopolis smiled widely. "In fact, it's everyone's problem. If that fraud Brack doesn't come up with the payment, then you, young lady, are out of a job."

Annie opened her mouth, but nothing came out except a tiny squeak.

The magician picked a piece of lint off his sleeve with one of his snow-white gloves. Charlie thought he looked dressed for a performance, with his perfect suit and long swirling cape.

"Is he right?" asked Annie. "Can he take away the hotel?"

Miranda Yu held her hand to her forehead as if she had a headache. "This is impossible," she said.

Walter Yu looked at Annie. "I'm afraid he may be right," he said. "Brack always makes payments at a certain time every month. It's part of the contract. And if he doesn't make a payment by tomorrow —"

"If he doesn't make the payment by tomorrow," interrupted Miranda Yu, "then the hotel is forfeit. In other words, the hotel would automatically change ownership."

"To me," finished the smug Theopolis. "It all

dates back to the very beginning of the hotel, when Abracadbra and I were dear friends."

"That's hard to believe," Charlie muttered.

"Friendship is a tricky thing," said Theopolis. "Especially between magicians. Especially when one magician steals a trick from another and . . ." He stopped. His ears were the color of ripe tomatoes. The magician cleared his throat, smoothed out his cape, and resumed his speech.

"Abracadabra and I were partners. He had the vision for this hotel. I had the cash. At the time, I was the world's most sought-after performer. I was planning a tour, and had no interest in overseeing the actual building. So I gave Brack the money, and he said he would repay me. Then I went on my tour and left this dreadful country behind."

"Brack did repay you," said Mrs. Yu. "He repays you every month, on time."

"Yes, dear lady," said Theopolis. "But as you know, our agreement includes an interesting clause in the contract. If Brack fails to make payments on this pile of bricks, then the ownership defaults to me."

"That's crazy," said Charlie. "Can't someone else make the payments for him? Like Mrs. Yu?"

"No," said the sneering magician. "The contract says that Abracadabra must pay. It must be his signature on the check. Or his skinny little fingers that hand over the cash. And, as an old friend, I would certainly give him a few days to make his payment, but . . . well, he doesn't seem to be around, does he?"

Theopolis's smile disappeared. "I shall be back tomorrow at this same time," he said. "And if Brack is still not here, then I shall expect your resignations within the week." He glanced around the lobby. "This used to be such a lovely place in its day. Ah, well, a renovation is clearly in order. And a more competent staff. Good day." With a swirl of his cape, he vanished into the shadows of the vast lobby.

Mr. Yu patted his wife's shoulder. "Don't worry, dear. We'll think of something."

Mrs. Yu glanced over at her husband. "I'm worried about Tyler. I've been beeping him for the past half hour."

Annie grabbed Charlie's hand and pulled him behind a pillar. "We have to find Brack right now!" she said. "And Tyler."

If not, Annie and Tyler and his parents would have to find new jobs, maybe a new home.

A crowd of people, carrying umbrellas and shaking the rain from their coats, entered the lobby from outside. A few photographers were flashing cameras and shoving microphones into wet, smiling faces.

Annie groaned. "I forgot all about the show."

"Another one?" Charlie asked.

"The real one. It starts in a couple hours, but people come early to get good seats."

Charlie grabbed Annie's hand. "Let's head up to the fourteenth floor. We haven't been there yet, and that's where the two magicians are staying."

Riding in the elevator, Annie complained about Theopolis. "He's such a snake!" she said. "The way he looks at people. Ew! And even his clothes. He dresses up like a big shot, like he's better than us."

Charlie's thoughts were elsewhere. Why did Theopolis want the hotel now? Did he need money? Was he no longer in demand as the world's most sought after performer?

"You're right, he did look awfully dressed up," said Charlie. "He even wore those white magician gloves." That made him think. "Did you notice anything else about his clothes?"

"Just that he looked like he was going onstage," said Annie, sourly.

"They were perfect," said Charlie.

"His clothes?"

"Perfectly dry."

Annie's eyes lit up. "There's a thunderstorm."

"A big thunderstorm," added Charlie. "There should have been some rain on his clothes. Or his shoes."

"And he didn't have an umbrella," Annie said. "He came from inside the hotel."

When Charlie thought about it, this whole mystery was all about where people were and when. He listed everything in his notebook.

? ? WHERE IS BRACK?! ? ?

1. Brack disappeared last night. Probably before rehearsal, or he would have been there. Sometime before 8 pm.

2. Dragonstone arrived at 8. He went straight to the rehearsal.

3. DeVille showed up this morning, after Tyler left for school. And according to Annie, DeVille had never been to the hotel before.

4. Theopolis showed up during a raging thunderstorm, but none of his clothes were wet.

When the elevator let them out on the fourteenth floor, Annie led Charlie toward the magicians' rooms.

"Did you really mean it when you said you knew how the trick was done?" said Annie. "The wormhole trick?"

"Sure," Charlie said. "I saw it on the blueprint. That glass door doesn't open. It has no hinges. But you can get around it."

"How?" Annie asked.

"It slides," said Charlie. "The glass can slide into the wall on either side, several inches at least."

"I still don't get it," Annie said.

Charlie frowned, trying to figure out how to explain the trick. "You noticed how skinny Dragonstone was, right?" he said. "He slid the door to one side and squeezed around it. Then he slid it back in place, grabbed the end of the ribbon, and tied it around his waist."

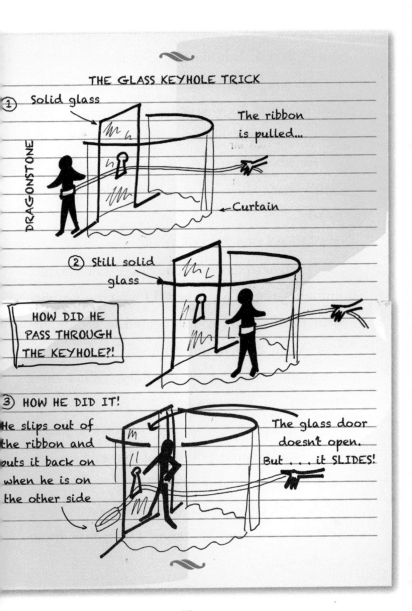

THE GLASS KEYHOLE TRICK

① Solid glass

The ribbon is pulled...

DRAGONSTONE

←Curtain

② Still solid glass

HOW DID HE PASS THROUGH THE KEYHOLE?!

③ HOW HE DID IT!

He slips out of the ribbon and puts it back on when he is on the other side

The glass door doesn't open. But . . . it SLIDES!

"Wow," said Annie. "It seems so easy when you explain it. Not like magic at all."

"I know," said Charlie. "Most tricks are like that once you know how they're done. Here, let me show you on the blueprint."

He reached into his backpack to gather the rolls. That's when he saw the folded piece of paper.

"What's that?" asked Annie.

"I forgot to show you one thing," said Charlie, unfolding the yellow paper. "I found this upstairs with Brack's stuff, too. I figured it was important. Magic carpets and stuff, see?"

Annie looked at it carefully. "What does 'turn lily' mean?" she asked.

"You're reading it wrong. That says 'Tiger lily here,'" said Charlie, pointing at the yellow paper. "I don't know what it means."

"I don't either, but it doesn't say that," Annie said. "It says 'Turn lily there.' Lilies. Like these on the wall."

Annie pointed to the flowery wallpaper.

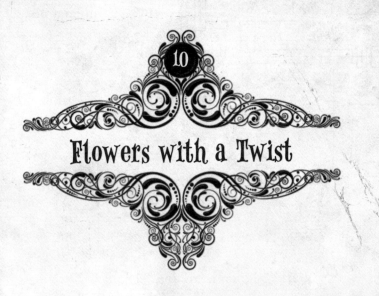

Flowers with a Twist

Charlie Hitchcock stared at the three words. It actually read TURN LILY THERE. Of course! Once you knew how to read it, the letters looked different, made another kind of sense. Charlie forgot that in order to solve a puzzle he needed to take into account unpredictable factors. And the most unpredictable factors were people.

Their likes and dislikes, their voice, their walk, their clothes, and even their handwriting.

"Annie, you're a genius!" said Charlie.

"I am?" she said, smiling. "Thanks."

"These lilies," Charlie said, pointing to the wallpaper. "They're not the same as the flowers down on the twelfth floor."

"No," said Annie. "Each floor has a different flower. Roses, lilies, tulips, violets. I think that was Mr. Brack's idea, because he really likes flowers."

"This writing is important," said Charlie, waving the yellow paper in his fist. "And it has something to do with the thirteenth floor, which is just below our feet. And something to do with a magic carpet. And whoever was visiting Brack last night saw his notes. These notes."

"So now what?" asked Annie.

"'Turn lily there,'" Charlie said. "I wonder where 'there' is? Well, we might as well head to the magicians' rooms. But let's keep an eye on the wallpaper. Maybe there's a hidden code or something."

As Annie led them toward the magicians' rooms, Charlie kept his eyes trained on the lilies that flowed past them on the wallpaper. He started feeling dizzy from staring at the repeating pattern of flowers.

"Here we are," said Annie. She had stopped between two doors. On the floor next to the wall lay several trays of half-eaten food, empty glasses, and a single coffee cup.

Charlie stuffed the yellow paper in his pocket. He felt something else.

The red hair.

The hair that matched the fake beard. If the hair was fake, then whoever was visiting Brack was in disguise. And no one would wear a disguise except someone who might be recognized.

"Theopolis!" said Charlie.

"Where?" said Annie, turning around.

"Upstairs, last night," said Charlie. "That's who visited Brack. He was the one who took the blueprints so he could get information about the hotel. And he's stayed inside the hotel ever since."

"But I thought Mr. Dragonstone and DeVille used the blueprints to figure out that trick with the glass door," said Annie.

"Yeah, you're right," said Charlie.

"So how did the blueprints get from Mr. Theopolis to the dressing room for Mr. Dragonstone?" she asked.

That's the big question, thought Charlie. *How did the blueprints get in there?*

"Charlie," Annie said slowly. "Look." She was pointing at the carpet.

There was a pattern in the carpet. A rectangle made of twisting lines of gold and turquoise and emerald and cream.

"It's beautiful," said Annie. "Like something out of the *Arabian Nights*."

"Yeah, like something from *Aladdin*," said Charlie. "It looks like —"

"A magic carpet," they said together.

DeVille's Trick

Charlie took a deep breath. "Remember what Brack wrote down."

"'Turn lily there,'" said Annie. They both turned to the wallpaper on either side of the hall and examined the painted flowers.

One of the lilies in the wall was not painted. It was actually a small plaster flower on the wallpaper itself, blending in with the two-dimensional flowers around it.

"I found it! I found it!" Annie said.

One of the magicians' doors opened abruptly. "Who is making all that noise?" A man stuck out his head and looked at Annie and Charlie. His expression was not kind.

His face made Charlie think of a million things all at once. He thought of the fake red beard. Someone in disguise having coffee with Brack last night. Someone reading Brack's writing as the old magician had been studying his precious blueprint. He thought of the signature on the card in Dragonstone's room. The writer had not written "The DeV." The writer had made a mistake. He'd started writing the wrong word — "Th" — and then changed his mind.

Then Charlie thought of the Glass Door trick. How the French wizard DeVille had told Ty to stand at the far end of the hall since he knew his way around there.

And how the man had shouted at Charlie, calling him "Hitchcock," and ordering him to pull aside the black curtains to reveal Dragonstone.

How did DeVille know that Ty worked at the hotel? They never saw each other. Ty had already left for school before the Frenchman arrived. And how did he know Charlie's last name?

How did DeVille know?

Because he had been to the hotel before. In fact, that's how the blueprint got from Theopolis to the dressing room. The same man who stole the papers also hid them. The same man who saw the blueprint last night saw it during the rehearsal, and then suggested the Glass Door and Wormhole finale to Dragonstone's Empty Straitjacket trick after the rehearsal.

Because he was the only person who knew the secret of the glass door besides Brack.

One person.

A single person behind two beards, one red and one black.

"Theopolis!" cried Charlie.

"You meddling little brat!" said the magician, stepping into the hall. "You're always ruining my plans!"

"When Dragonstone called you, his friend 'DeVille,' to substitute for Brack, you were already inside the hotel," said Charlie.

"I'll make sure you never leave this hotel again," said Theopolis. "I'll deal with you like I dealt with Brack!"

"You're angry with him just because he revealed one of your tricks?" said Charlie. He was stalling for time.

"Just? Just?!" The magician's face contorted with rage. "A magician's tricks are his life. I was never able to use that trick again."

"You've never stolen a trick?" asked Annie.

Theopolis laughed. "I may have borrowed one or two. But I transform them. In my hands they become true miracles."

Charlie and Annie heard a sound behind

them in the hall. "This is great," came a voice. "Just what I need for my scoop." Joey Bingham stepped out of the shadows. He held a video camera aimed at the arguing trio.

"Young man," said Theopolis. "Have you been recording all this time?"

"Mostly," said Joey with a big grin. "Keep talking. This is great stuff."

"What're you doing here?" Charlie asked.

"I've been here all day," said Joey. "I kept seeing you two running around and always going back to the elevator. I knew something was up." He laughed. "Up? Get it?"

Theopolis completely changed his manner. He became smooth and friendly. He sleeked his hair and bowed toward the camera. "Would you like a quick interview before the big show?" he said. "Learn how a famous performer prepares for the stage?"

"No," said Charlie. "You want something better than that, Joey. Something more exclusive.

Something amazing. Something like how a magic trick is performed."

"No!" said Theopolis.

"Yeah," said Joey.

"Like the secret of the falling magician," Charlie said. "How did Dragonstone disappear from his straitjacket and then end up on the twelfth floor?"

Theopolis took a step toward the boys. "You're just like that thief Brack!" he snarled.

Charlie faced Joey's camera and spoke as quickly as could. "The secret is simple," Charlie said. "There's a second straitjacket stuck to the back of the real one Dragonstone wears. He probably has a string or flap he can secretly pull with his hand. When he falls, the second jacket pops off and falls toward the stage. Dragonstone, still inside the first one, falls behind a trick mirror onstage. They both hit the ground at the same time."

"It looked like a cool trick," said Annie.

"It was," said Charlie. "And is. Dragonstone needs to be very skilled at timing, and at falling. He probably lands on some kind of safety net behind the trick mirrors. But it takes a lot of skill to fall and not break your neck."

Annie smiled. "And didn't you tell me earlier how Dragonstone passed through that solid glass door, too?"

"Enough, enough!" cried the magician. He folded his arms and looked down at Charlie. "What do you want?" he asked.

"I don't want anything," said Charlie. "But I'm sure Brack would like to keep his hotel."

"The hotel is mine," shouted the magician. "And so is that video camera!"

Another door popped open. A tall, red-headed man appeared. He stepped into the hall pulling on a pair of gloves.

"What's all this noise?" asked David Dragonstone. "Monsieur DeVille! You aren't dressed for the performance yet."

"Will there be a performance, Mr. DeVille?" asked Charlie.

Dragonstone froze. He stared at Theopolis. "What does he mean, DeVille?"

Charlie whispered to Theopolis, "If Brack doesn't have a hotel, then you don't have a trick. Joey and I will play his video to the audience that's waiting for you downstairs."

"Think you're clever, don't you, Mr. Hitchcock?" said Theopolis. "Very well. You have won this battle." He turned and walked back to the door of his room. He stopped and shot Charlie a wicked glance. "But the war is not over!" And with a snap of his teeth, he exited the hall.

"Wish I could stay and chat with you youngsters, but I have to be onstage in twenty minutes," said Dragonstone. He hurried down the hall toward the elevators.

"Wow!" said Joey, turning toward Annie and Charlie. "That was incredible! What a scoop!"

"You can't show people your video," said Charlie.

"I know that," said Joey. "I need that magician guy to sign a release form first."

"No," said Charlie. "I mean you can't show it ever. Or Brack loses the hotel."

Annie smiled. "Let's go downstairs to watch the show. And then Charlie and I can explain everything that's been going on."

"You got a deal," said Joey.

As they walked back down the hallway, Charlie glanced at the magic carpet design beneath their shoes. A gleaming rectangle of many colors.

He knew the rectangle held the secret to finding his missing friends.

He also knew that as soon as he and Annie had convinced Joey Bingham not to show his video, they'd get right back on that elevator again.

They had to find the thirteenth floor of the Hocus Pocus Hotel.

Shifting Shadows

Charlie had never slept in a magician's house before. It was disappointing.

No unearthly moans.

No rattling chains.

No phantoms flitting through walls.

Charlie would have welcomed them, and would have spent the rest of the night trying to solve the mystery of what they really were. He loved solving puzzles.

Charlie yawned and pulled the blanket to his chin. Counting ghosts would have been a lot more fun than lying there counting sheep. Instead, he listened to the rumbling of the thunderstorm outside and to the ticking of a grandfather clock.

The clock faced the sofa on which he was trying to fall asleep. A flash of lightning lit up the dial.

Almost three o'clock? he thought. *Only four more hours!* He groaned and rolled over, gazing around Brack's sitting room.

Groans came from the closet.

For a nanosecond, Charlie hoped it was a ghost, but he knew the sound was just old floorboards settling in the storm.

The boy glanced over at the magician's big, wooden desk. The pile of books and papers

covering the desk was the reason he was staying overnight.

On the magician's desk lay a clue that Charlie hoped would lead him to his friends. It was a sheet of paper that held an unusual list of words:

It was the last entry in the list that bothered him the most. *The 12.* Did that mean the twelfth floor?

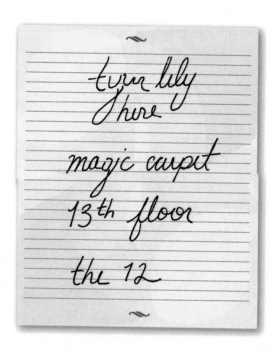

Then why hadn't Brack written it the way he wrote *13th floor* just above it?

Dnnng! Dnnng! Dnnng!

Three o'clock. Charlie shifted on the sofa and pulled the blanket around him more tightly.

What — or who — are the Twelve? he wondered. There were twelve months in the year. Twelve numbers on a clock. Twelve days of Christmas. Twelve signs of the *Zzzzz* . . .

Brack's sitting room soon echoed with the thunder-like rumbling of Charlie's snores.

And while the boy slept, a dark figure — waiting patiently in the shadows — slipped from the closet, made its way to the front door, and darted away from the magician's house.

* * *

Four hours later, Charlie yawned and stepped off the elevator, shuffling through the vast lobby of the Abracadabra.

"Charlie! Over here!" came a voice.

Charlie rubbed his eyes and saw Annie waving furiously near the front desk. Another girl stood next to her.

"Charlie," said Annie, smiling widely. "This is Cozette. She's new here. Just started a couple weeks ago."

The other girl held up a hand and said, "Hey." She had thick dark hair and bright eyes, and wore pink shoes that matched her fingernail polish.

"Cozette's going to help us," said Annie. "I figured two heads are better than one, and, well, three heads are better than two."

Before Charlie could ask a question, Annie grabbed his hand and pulled him, along with Cozette, toward the hotel restaurant. "Come on, I'm starving," she said.

Tyler's dad, Walter Yu, showed them to a table. "Breakfast is on the house," he said. "Thanks to you, Annie, and your friend here, we can all keep our jobs. And the hotel is safe!"

Cozette looked puzzled, so Annie said, "I'll explain it all later."

And she did, with help from Charlie, while the three of them dug into eggs, toast, bacon, and fruit.

Annie explained how the two of them, but mostly Charlie, had saved the hotel from falling into the hands of Theopolis.

"That snake threatened to take away the Hocus Pocus if Mr. Brack didn't pay the rent," said Annie.

"But Mr. Brack is missing," said Cozette.

Annie and Charlie nodded. Charlie had kept Theopolis from stealing the hotel. But who knew how long that would keep the evil magician quiet? Charlie was afraid the man would come up with another awful plan. And soon.

"That's why we have to find Brack," said Charlie.

"And Tyler, too," added Annie. "They're both in trouble."

"We told Ty's parents that he's been helping us look for Brack," said Charlie. "But if we don't find him soon, Mrs. Yu's going to get suspicious.

"You should call the police," said Cozette.

"We will," said Annie. "Tomorrow. If we still can't find them by the end of the day. But we know they're somewhere in the hotel."

"On the thirteenth floor," said Charlie.

"Thirteen?" said Cozette. Her eyes grew wide. "That seems unlucky."

"But we'll go to the fourteenth floor first," said Charlie.

"Right," said Annie. "The lily."

Cozette put down her fork. "Lily who?"

"No, it's lily what," said Annie. "A flower."

"But not really a flower," said Charlie.

Cozette sighed. "I don't know why you talked me into this, Annie."

"Because we have to help Tyler," said her friend. Cozette and Charlie shared a glance. They knew Annie liked Tyler. Really liked him.

Cozette patted her lips with her napkin and then dropped it on the table. "Okay then," she said. "Let's go rescue Tyler."

When they got off the elevator at the fourteenth floor, Charlie led them to the hallway he and Annie had investigated the day before. Annie waved toward two doors, side by side. "That's where the magicians are staying this week. Theopolis there, and Mr. Dragonstone there."

"David Dragonstone?" said Cozette. "He is so cute! Do you think he'll come out if we knock on the door? Will he be wearing his white suit?"

"We're here to look for Tyler, remember?" said Annie.

"Besides, David Dragonstone might be involved in this," added Charlie.

"Charlie figured out how Mr. Dragonstone did his magic tricks," said Annie. "Figured it all out by himself. Well, except for one thing, that is."

"What's that?" asked Cozette.

"The trick where he walks through a glass door down on the twelfth floor," Annie said. "Charlie knows how he got through the glass. But he doesn't know how he got to the twelfth floor in the first place."

Charlie walked down the hall.

"Tyler stood at one end of that hallway. The solid glass door was at the other end. But somehow Dragonstone appeared in the middle," he said.

"How?" asked Cozette.

Charlie was staring carefully at the wall. "I think it has something to do with this."

The two girls rushed over to him.

"That's the lily!" said Annie. The dark wallpaper was covered with patterns of lilies. The flower Charlie was staring at, however, was not printed on the wallpaper. It was made of plaster and sat on top of the paper, in three dimensions, but blended in with the flowers around it. If a

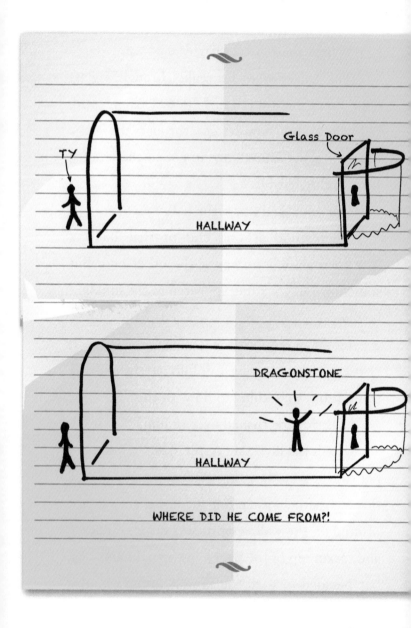

person hadn't been looking for it, they would have overlooked it in the flowing pattern.

"Brack's writing," said Charlie, referring to the paper he had found the day before, "had the words 'turn lily there.'"

"I figured out that part," said Annie.

"So, how do we turn it?" asked Cozette.

"I'm not exactly sure," said Charlie. He took a few steps back for a better view. On the floor beneath his shoes was a rectangle. It was the only shape in the otherwise plain, red carpet. A rectangle made of twisting lines of gold and emerald and cream. Charlie was sure that the two items that didn't fit in, the rectangle and the flower, were parts of the same puzzle.

Cozette shrugged. "Why don't you just try turning it?"

She reached out and grabbed the plaster lily. With a small crunch, it turned in her grip like a doorknob.

Something thudded in the hallway and shook

the floor. Annie gasped. The rectangle in the carpet tilted downward, like a waterslide, into a dark rectangular space. The last things Charlie saw were Cozette's pink shoes.

He fell through the floor, then rolled into something hard. With another thump, the carpet above him tilted back up and the light disappeared.

Charlie heard a wrenching sound, a scream, and then nothing. He was in darkness.

The Thirteenth Floor

True, deep darkness.

Charlie felt his heart pumping faster. He started breathing harder.

Then he heard something.

. . . beep . . . beep . . .

"Ty, is that you?" he called.

"Yeah, it's my stupid beeper," came Tyler's

familiar voice. "It's gone off about a million times. If my parents had given me a phone, then maybe I could have called them and gotten out of this hole, but no, I'm not responsible enough. Even though I do all the work around here."

The darkness in front of Charlie's eyes appeared to swirl. A shadow separated from the others. A silhouette.

"You've been on the thirteenth floor the whole time?" asked Charlie.

"Yeah, and I'm not the only one, brainiac. Brack's here too. But I think he's hurt."

"You think? Don't you know?"

"I can't see him," said Ty.

Charlie's heart began beating harder again. "There's no lights in here?!" he said.

"Well, there aren't any windows on this floor, but there's a few lights. But that's not the problem. He's locked behind a door and neither of us can open it. So I've been looking for a way out for hours!"

Light burst above them. Charlie could see that he and Ty were sitting in a hall that resembled the others in the hotel.

The secret rectangular door had re-opened overhead and slanted toward them. Annie and Cozette ran down the carpeted ramp.

"Tyler!" exclaimed Annie. "I'm so glad you're all right."

"Yeah!" said Ty. "Now we can get out of here."

But as soon as the two girls stepped off the ramp, it sprang quickly back into place, and out of reach.

"Don't worry," said Charlie. "I think I know how we can get out of here."

"You do?" said Ty. "Then why did you take so long? I've been starving!"

"I waited so long because I just figured it out," answered Charlie. "It's not like we haven't been trying."

"*We* just figured it out," said Cozette. "I was the one who turned that weirdo lily thing."

"Right," Charlie said. "We. Sorry."

"*We* need to get Brack," said Ty.

"I've got a phone," said Cozette. She turned it on and its pale blue light helped guide them through the hallway.

Tyler looked the way he always did. Spiky black hair, jeans, boots, and a scowl on his face. He stopped in front of a door. "We have a slight problem," he said.

"Now what?" asked Annie.

"The door is locked," Ty said. "And Brack's inside."

"I have a passkey!" Charlie said. He pulled the keycard out of his pocket.

Charlie heard a low moan from the other side of the door. "Brack!" he called. "It's us!" Cozette's phone light made it bright enough to see the door.

Charlie looked at the door, and then stopped. "Uh, where's the slot for the passkey?" The old wooden door had a traditional lock and keyhole.

"These old doors don't have the new electronic system," said Annie. "We need an old-school metal key."

"And that's probably been missing for fifty years," said Charlie, groaning.

"Now that you mention it," said Annie, "there are some old keys hanging behind the desk."

"You mean these?" asked Cozette. She held out a small ring of dark metal keys.

"How did you —?" Annie started.

"I figured if we were going into the old part of the Hocus Pocus, we might need them," said Cozette.

"You're smarter than you look," said Ty.

"Stand aside," said Cozette. She tried a few of the keys in the lock. Finally, there was a click.

The door opened, and in the phone's blue light, they saw a closet door just inside.

"Brack!" called Ty.

A groan came from within the closet. Ty

twisted a deadbolt knob on the door and opened it. The four companions saw an old man on the floor inside, his thin back against the wall, his wrinkled face stretched in a grimace of pain.

The Twelve

"Master Hitchcock!" said the man in a tired, raspy voice. "And Master Yu. And Miss Solo."

"How are you, Brack?" asked Charlie.

"Body and soul still together, young man," said Brack, pushing himself into a better position. "And this charming young woman must be Miss Bailey."

Cozette stared. "You know who I am?" she said. "I've only worked here a few weeks."

"We need to get you out of here," said Ty.

"Carefully," said Brack. "I think I may have sprained an ankle."

"Who did this to you?" said Charlie.

"I have an idea," said Brack. "But I don't have any evidence, of course. It was dark when I woke up here. The last thing I remember was sitting in my house."

"With Theopolis!" said Charlie.

Brack blinked, surprised. "Why, yes. At least, that's who he turned out to be. He was wearing a disguise."

"A red beard," said Annie.

"Somebody better explain what's been going on," said Ty. "And I mean now."

"First things first," said Brack. He lifted a shaking hand and pointed. "I believe there's a men's room in that direction. I could hear the pipes through the wall."

Ty gently hoisted Brack to his feet and hunkered under one of the older man's shoulders. Charlie and Annie supported him on the other side. Cozette raised her phone and a door loomed out of the darkness. While Ty helped Brack walk inside, the other three turned and gasped.

A hand reached out toward them. Icy white fingers. Annie screamed. Charlie couldn't speak. Ty stepped out of the bathroom, closing the door behind him. "What's going on?" he asked.

Cozette pointed. The clutching white fingers hadn't moved. They could see the hand was attached to a bare white arm that led to a naked shoulder.

"Look out!" said Ty. As Cozette's light traveled up the mysterious white shape, Ty saw another figure close behind.

Neither of the white shadows moved. "Who are you?" Ty demanded.

The four companions jumped as something

moved behind them. It was Brack, who had opened the bathroom door and was grasping the side of the doorway for balance. "I'm afraid he can't answer you," he said. "None of them can."

Cozette lifted her light. They saw more and more figures crowded in front of them.

All pale, all frozen in place, all silent.

"Statues," said Charlie.

Brack nodded. "They are the great secret of the thirteenth floor," he said. "A secret I thought was a rumor until I saw them just now with my own eyes."

"Who are they?" asked Ty.

"The Twelve," said Brack.

Charlie looked closer at the blurry, bluish shapes in the cellphone's gleam. One of them brandished a sword. Another held a spear with three sharp prongs. A female figure wore an old-fashioned helmet and carried a shield.

I've seen them before, thought Charlie. He had a memory that held onto images like a computer

hard drive. "Acute visual memory," his teachers called it. Other people might call it a photographic memory.

Once Charlie saw a picture or a movie or a show, he never forgot it. For example, the photo he had seen in an old book at the library of some statues. The same statues he'd seen on a show on the History Channel.

"The Twelve Olympians," said Charlie.

"You mean, like athletes?" asked Annie,

Ty rolled his eyes. "Like the Greek gods," he said. "*Clash of the Titans*, The Immortals, Percy Jackson."

"You read?" said Cozette in a quiet voice.

Ty ignored her. "That must be Ares," he said, pointing at the statue with the sword.

"And there's Poseidon and Athena," said Charlie. He saw a statue of a beautiful woman with long hair, holding a stone apple in her cold marble hand. "That one is Aphrodite, the goddess of beauty."

"Yeah," said Ty. "Some dude gave her that apple because she was the prettiest."

"The Twelve," said Brack. "These statues were a gift to the hotel many, many years ago. They were the handiwork of a famous Spanish sculptor, Ernesto Endriago."

"One guy made them?" asked Cozette.

"One very talented guy, yes," said Brack. "He sent them to the hotel as a gift. He came from a long line of magicians — he was the only sculptor, and a disappointment to his father. But these magnificent statues were delivered here and then forgotten. I knew they had been sent, but never saw them. It was a very busy time. Deliverymen must have put them on this floor by mistake."

"Wow," said Annie. "So, we're like the first people to see them since Ernesto!"

"Where were they supposed to go?" asked Charlie.

"Endriago designed them to be installed

on the roof," said Brack. "The twelve gods of Greek mythology gazing down on humans from on high. Just as they once did from Mount Olympus."

"Awesome," said Tyler.

"Awesome indeed, but it wasn't a good idea," said Brack. "They're far too valuable to be exposed to the elements."

"Um, how valuable?" said Charlie.

"Endriago was killed in the Second World War," Brack said. "These are the last — and the greatest — works from his hand. They must be priceless."

Charlie wondered how much a single statue would cost. A million? A hundred million? That would pay for the hotel a thousand times over. Brack would be able to pay for the whole thing, and Theopolis would be out of his life forever.

Charlie was too busy thinking about dollar signs to notice the shadowy figure moving beyond the circle of light cast from Cozette's phone. It moved from the statue of Apollo to Hermes, and then hid behind Hades, the lord of the dead. Then it smiled.

The Old Magic Returns

Tyler sighed. "I'm starving here, people. And we need a doctor to look at Brack's ankle."

Cozette turned to Charlie. "You said you knew a way out of here."

"Right," said Charlie. "Let's go back to the hall we first landed in."

It took longer to retrace their steps with the

injured Brack, but soon they were back in the hallway.

"See?" said Charlie, pointing to the floor. "I knew it was there." In the glow of the phone they saw a familiar shape on the carpet.

"Aladdin's magic carpet," said Annie. "Or at least it looks like it."

"Just like the rectangle above us, on the fourteenth floor," said Charlie.

"You mean it was right there all the time?" said Ty.

Charlie began running his hands along the wall, searching for another hidden switch. "I figured they'd be right on top of each other," he said. "Ah, here it is." His left hand touched a bumpy shape protruding from the wallpaper.

Another flower. This one was a sunflower. "Stand back," he yelled. Then he twisted the plaster flower just as Cozette had twisted the lily.

Something banged against the floor. Gears rattled and walls shook as the floor began to sag.

Light shot up from below as the rectangle in the carpet slanted downward to reveal a lit hallway on the twelfth floor.

Carefully, they helped Brack down the ramp. As soon as they all stepped into the lower hallway, the ramp snapped up like the end of a teeter-totter.

"This is the hallway with the glass door," said Ty. "This is where I went up. After you took off for the elevators, the ramp came down again."

"So why didn't you just come back the same way?" asked Annie.

"I didn't know how it worked," said Ty.

"Well, that's how David Dragonstone got into the hallway without you seeing him enter it," said Charlie. "Remember how you said you saw the black curtains dropping down over the glass door? That's what clued me in to this secret ramp. The black curtains used in the magic trick moved from side to side, on a frame, like regular curtains. When you said you saw them

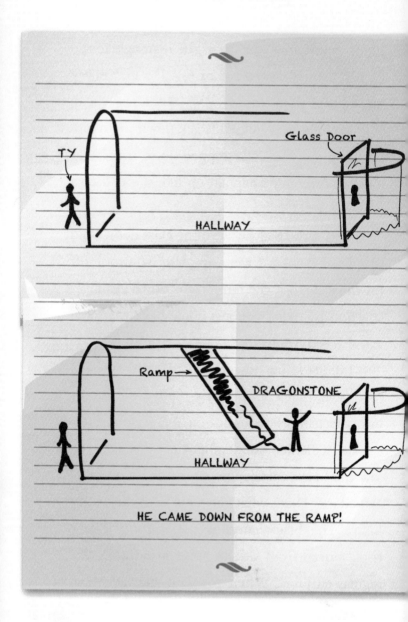

HE CAME DOWN FROM THE RAMP!

drop down, from the far end of the hall where you were standing, I knew you must have seen something else dropping down."

"After you left the hall, I took one last look around," said Ty. "And then, for no reason, the ceiling began to open up, and the ramp came down. That's when I went up to the thirteenth floor and got stuck. Hey, how many of those ramps are there?" he asked Brack.

"I don't know," said Brack. "I hired architects and builders who were magicians, you know. The hotel has magic built into the very walls. Even I don't know all of the Abracadabra's secrets."

They led Brack to the elevators on the twelfth floor and descended to the main floor lobby.

"Ty!" shouted his mother as soon as they stepped into the lobby. Miranda Yu rushed over, her arms outspread. She gave Ty a hug, but he shrugged it off.

Mrs. Yu's expression grew stern and she

folded her arms. "Tyler Yu. Why have you been ignoring your beeper for the past twenty-four hours?" she demanded.

Brack raised his hands. "I'm afraid that was all my fault, Mrs. Yu. Tyler was busy rescuing me."

Once the magician explained how Tyler had been trying to help him, and how he had hurt his ankle during his abduction, Miranda Yu's anger drained away. She ordered Brack to wait in the lobby while she phoned a doctor.

Brack settled into a plump, overstuffed chair. Meanwhile, Cozette peppered Annie with dozens of questions about David Dragonstone and whether they could go back upstairs for his autograph. A flash of lightning blazed through the vast lobby. It flickered on a forest of columns and a jungle of potted plants.

"I thought that storm was over," said Charlie.

"We all make mistakes," came a booming voice from the center of the room. "I heard the wonderful news of your return, old friend," said Theopolis, bowing toward the seated Brack.

"We just got here," said Charlie. "How could you have heard anything?"

Theopolis slowly shook his head. "Still doubting my mystical abilities, I see," he said. "Well, Brack, I'm so glad you haven't left us. For good, I mean. Oh, I was so worried."

"Did you really think I would leave this place?" asked Brack with a grim smile.

"Never," said Theopolis. "I know how much this stuffy old fleabag means to you. In fact, I know exactly how much."

Yeah. Down to the penny, I bet, thought Charlie.

"And now that you're back," said Theopolis, "you must attend one of David Dragonstone's performances. It would mean so much to the young man to have one of magic's oldest practitioners in the audience."

"I have heard all about Dragonstone's tricks from my young friends," said Brack.

"Well," said Theopolis, giving Charlie a sour smile. "Don't believe everything you hear. Ah well, you're here, these brats are here, and everything is back to normal. Charming. I must talk to my partner about his next show. We're planning something really big."

"I can't wait," said Brack.

Theopolis swirled his cape and strode toward the elevators. "How can Brack just sit there and not say anything to that weasel?" said Ty. "He didn't even ask that creep for an apology for locking him in that room."

Charlie straightened his shirt. "Like Brack said, he doesn't have any evidence against Theopolis," he said. "I mean, Brack didn't exactly see who trapped him on the thirteenth floor."

"Then we're gonna find evidence," said Ty. "Yeah, that's it. I know how to catch him red-handed." Ty looked down at Charlie. "Come on, Hitchcock. We're going back to the thirteenth floor."

"What?" squawked Charlie.

"The Twelve," said Ty. "Those statues. You heard Brack say they were priceless. I'll bet that's what Theopolis is up to. He's gonna steal them and make millions. But we're gonna sit in that room and grab him as soon as he makes his move."

This time they brought flashlights. Annie had to help Mrs. Yu in the office with some paperwork, so Charlie, Ty, and Cozette returned to the fourteenth floor, to the hallway outside Dragonstone and Theopolis's bedrooms.

After fiddling with the plaster lily a few dozen times, they were able to keep the ramp stuck in a diagonal position.

Once they stepped down to the thirteenth floor, they did the same with the sunflower and the second ramp.

Now both ramps were stuck in the "down" position, and light flooded into the old, hidden hallway from above and below.

"The door's over there, around the corner," said Ty. "Room 1308."

Their flashlights were able to pick out more details of the fantastic statues.

"Who's the lady in the helmet?" asked Cozette.

Charlie joined her. "That's Athena. Also called Minerva. The goddess of wisdom."

"Why would a smart woman need a helmet and a shield?" asked Cozette.

"Because she was smart," said Ty. "There were a lot of crazy, scary dudes back in the Greek days."

"And who's this with the wings on his feet?" Cozette asked.

"He's one of my favorites," said Charlie. "He's Hermes, the messenger of the gods. The wings helped him travel back and forth between Mount Olympus and Earth."

"Hitchcock has a favorite Greek god?" Tyler said, smirking. "Nerd alert."

"He looks cute," said Cozette.

"Hitchcock?!" said Ty.

Cozette's face flushed deep red. "No! The messenger guy."

Charlie's face felt hot. He quickly tried changing the subject by pointing at the statue of a tall male holding a bow. A quiver of arrows hung at his back, and a small sun beamed from his brow. "That's Apollo. He's supposed to be the god of the sun and beauty and —"

"Who's this creepy guy?" asked Ty.

Charlie and Cozette walked over to the statue Ty was facing. In the small space with all the statues' bodies jammed together, it was hard to see them all at once.

"I'm not sure," said Charlie. "But I think he's Hades. The god of the underworld."

Cozette shivered. "You mean, like dead people and stuff? I'm getting out of here."

Ty turned to her. "I thought you wanted to help us guard this place."

"You guys guard it. I have work to do," said Cozette. "Besides, these statues aren't going anywhere. They weigh a ton."

To prove her wrong, Ty bent his knees, grasped Hades, and tried straightening up. He strained and grunted, and did manage to shift the statue from its base slightly.

"See? No sweat," said Tyler, wiping his forehead.

"Like I said, they weigh a ton," replied Cozette.

"Wait a minute, Cozette," said Charlie. "So, Ty, what exactly is your plan? What do you want us to do?"

Tyler stared at Charlie as if he had just arrived on the planet. "Stand. Guard. Over. The. Statues," he said. "And catch that creep Theopolis when he comes in to steal them."

"Stay up here?" said Cozette.

"We'll take turns," said Ty. "You wimps go do your work, or read more books, or talk about your favorite gods. And I'll stay up here, with the door locked. Then you come back in an hour, and Charlie takes over. Bring plenty to eat. See if you can get my dad to make a pizza."

Tyler hurried him out of the room. A moment later, Cozette was also rushed into the hall, the door closing behind her. She turned, as if to re-enter, but the doorknob jiggled uselessly in her hand.

Cozette sighed. "Let's go back to the elevators and . . ." She hesitated. Charlie guessed she was thinking about how close they were to David Dragonstone's room.

"Did you hear something?" asked Cozette. "Like a thump or something?"

Charlie tried the knob, but the door was locked. The two of them pounded on the door. "Let us in!" shouted Charlie.

Not a sound came from the room of statues.

The Locked Door

Cozette handed Charlie her set of keys while she used her phone to call for help.

"The key's not working, Cozette," said Charlie.

"Tyler must have turned the deadbolt," said Cozette. "I don't see a keyhole for that."

"I hope someone comes soon," Charlie said.

Annie and Rocky were the first to arrive. Rocky Brown was a teenage boy with long blond hair who also worked at the front desk. Charlie quickly explained what happened.

"Stand back," said Rocky. He rammed into the door with his shoulder. It wouldn't give.

"That only works on TV," said Cozette.

"I just need a little more momentum," said Rocky. "Now, look out. I don't want you guys to get hurt." He took several steps back, drew in a deep breath, and then ran toward the door. His shoulder slammed into the wood like a linebacker tackling a tight end. The frame shattered and splinters flew into the hall. "I broke my shoulder!" Rocky screamed.

Charlie and Cozette beamed their flashlights into the darkness.

"Tyler!" cried Annie.

Just inside the room, on the floor, lay the motionless body of Tyler Yu.

"Could someone call a doctor?" asked Rocky.

He sat out in the hall, holding his left shoulder.

Then, things became even more confusing. Over Rocky's groans and Annie's cries, Charlie heard more people arriving. Walter and Miranda Yu shoved their way to the door. Brack hobbled in on a cane. Theopolis and David Dragonstone, obviously alerted by the noises drifting up to their rooms through the open ramp, joined the crowd. Charlie heard some of the hotel's residents as well, ex-magicians and performers like Mr. Madagascar, Dottie Drake, and the reclusive juggler Mr. Thursday, who had just moved into the hotel the week before.

Charlie found himself in the room, kneeling over Tyler, although he didn't remember how he got there. And as he glanced up, he saw more and more onlookers stepping through the broken doorframe and entering the dark room that had been unused for fifty years.

"Oh my dear, is that Tyler?"

"Is he alive?"

"What are all these statues doing here?"

"What is this place?"

"He's breathing. He's breathing!"

"I think I'm going to faint. Do you think the floor is clean enough?" That was Dottie Drake, at one time a famous magician's assistant. Her silver hair was swept up in a tall pile and she clutched her throat in terror. "Oh, that poor boy," she said. "The poor boy. I really do feel faint."

"Everyone move back!" yelled Miranda Yu. Even in an emergency she looked cool and professional. "And no fainting!" she said. "We don't have time for that. Someone call a doctor. The rest of you, wait outside."

Out in the hall, the scene reminded Charlie of a dentist's waiting room.

Except for the crying.

Annie was weeping softly as Dottie Drake hugged her. And Rocky was weeping rather loudly.

Charlie stared at Theopolis, but the magician would not meet his gaze.

I know he has something to do with this, thought Charlie. *But I need evidence. How did he do it? How did he get into a locked room with Ty, when Cozette and I were standing right outside the door? And — more importantly — how did he get back out?*

Wait!

Charlie stood up. He grabbed his flashlight and headed back inside the room. Mrs. Yu was sitting on the floor, gently rubbing Tyler's back. Her head snapped up. "Outside, Charlie," she ordered.

"But I have to look at something —"

"Out," she repeated.

Charlie had learned early on not to mess with the Yus. They all meant business, each in their own way. He stood for a moment, gripping his flashlight, not saying a word. He simply looked at Tyler's motionless body.

He had never seen the boy so quiet, so

vulnerable. It was like looking at a fallen soldier. Above Ty's body stood the statue of Ares with his outstretched sword.

Then Charlie turned and walked out, just as the ambulance team was hurrying in with their bags and a stretcher.

No Way Out

Once Tyler and Rocky had been taken away on stretchers by the EMTs, the hallway emptied quickly.

A half hour later, the last ones remaining were Charlie, Brack, and Mr. Yu, who frowned, examining the splintered door frame.

"I can't leave it like this," he muttered. "What a terrible accident."

"I don't believe it was an accident at all," said Brack. "Do you still have your flashlight, Charlie?"

Charlie nodded. He didn't need to hear another word from the old magician. He turned on his light and stepped into the room. Back and forth, he swung the flashlight's beam.

It was a single open room, a large hotel room with only ancient gods and spiderwebs for guests. He saw the statues. He saw the door to the bathroom that Brack and Tyler had both used. He saw a few pieces of old furniture. He saw an open space that was probably supposed to have been a closet but never had a door attached to it. The one thing that Charlie did not see in the glare of his flashlight: another door or window.

"Do you see what's missing?" whispered Brack.

"Yeah," said Charlie. "No way out."

"That's not what I meant," said Brack. "Something else."

Charlie swung the light some more. What else was not there that should have been? Did Brack mean — no, it was impossible.

Charlie used the flashlight as a spotlight on each of the Twelve. Zeus, Hera, Poseidon, Ares, Hermes, Apollo, Athena, Hades, Artemis, Demeter, Hephestus, and . . .

Where was the beautiful woman holding the apple? He counted them a second time.

"Aphrodite is missing," Charlie said. "But, Brack, how could that be? I saw Aphrodite when we first came in to get you."

"I saw her too, Charlie," he replied. "But someone got to her."

Charlie shut his eyes. He tried to think back. When he first entered the room, he had seen all of the Twelve, even if he saw a few only out of the corner of his eye. He could count them all.

And then he pictured the second time he came back, with Ty and Cozette. He remembered how crowded it had felt, walking through the forest of frozen figures in the stuffy room. But, yes, he had counted then, too.

There had been twelve gods and goddesses of stone. He was sure of it. They sometimes seemed to twitch and blink in the moving beams of light from the flashlights and Cozette's phone. The muscles in their fingers flexed, the veins in their necks pulsed. But there had been the Twelve.

Where was the goddess of beauty? She couldn't walk out on her carved, stone feet.

Or could she? Maybe that sculptor, Ernesto Endriago, was a magician after all. Maybe he possessed some genius skill for building stone figures that moved on their own.

But that still didn't solve the bigger mystery. How did Ty's attacker — and the statue — leave the room if it was locked from the inside? And while Charlie and Cozette stood guard outside?

"My stupid ankle!" cried Brack. "If only I hadn't hurt it, this wouldn't have happened! The statue would still be here."

"You don't think it was alive too, do you?" whispered Charlie. But Brack didn't answer. He just stared at the statues.

Mr. Yu was standing outside by the broken door frame. Charlie could hear him on his phone trying to get a carpenter and a locksmith to the hotel as quickly as possible.

Then he heard him talking to his wife, telling her that he would soon join her at the hospital.

"You don't, do you?" repeated Charlie. "Think it was alive?"

A stone cold shiver ran down Charlie's spine. The air in the dark room grew darker. He thought the statues were shuffling closer.

Don't blink, thought Charlie. *Keep an eye on them.*

Brack smiled. "Magic can always be explained," he said. "You've proven that before,

Master Hitchcock, time and again. And this can be explained too. I know that you'll solve this mystery, just as you have the others."

I'm not so sure about that, thought Charlie. He looked into Brack's eyes, and the feeling that the statues crowded in on him faded away. But his doubts remained. There was only one thing he was sure about. He couldn't let his friends down.

The Third Flower

How does a human get into a locked room? Charlie asked himself. *With a key.* A light went on in Charlie's brain.

Key!

He needed to ask Cozette about her rings of keys, and why they didn't work when he tried unlocking the door to help Tyler.

Charlie imagined Tyler, lying in a hospital room. The last time he had seen Tyler, the other boy was trying to lift the Hades statue. And he did, sort of. It was heavy, but not impossible to lift. If you had help.

"Brack," said Charlie. "How did those statues get here in the first place? I mean, they're heavy."

Brack paused, both hands gripping the top of his cane. "Well, I'm sure Endriago had them shipped here from Spain."

Charlie shook his head. "I mean, here. This floor. Those statues are heavy."

"Most of the heavy objects, like furniture for the guests rooms, were hauled up on the freight elevator at the rear of the hotel," Brack explained.

Charlie knew that the hotel's elevators didn't stop at the thirteenth floor.

But he wasn't so sure about the freight elevators. He hadn't seen them or used them before. That reminded him of the blueprints he'd found while looking for clues. They showed every part of the hotel. Charlie slipped his backpack off his shoulder and dug inside.

"Recognize these?," he said proudly to Brack, pulling out the big roll of paper.

"My blueprints!" the old man exclaimed.

"I found them in the magicians' dressing room backstage," said Charlie. He had discovered them the day before while searching for clues to Brack's disappearance.

Charlie pulled out the huge sheet that showed the 3D version of the entire Abracadabra Hotel. Each floor of the hotel was outlined in faint white lines against a blue background. Every hall, every room could be seen.

"Here's where we are now," Charlie said, pointing to the page.

"And here are the freight elevators in back," said Brack, indicating a tall vertical tube at the back of the hotel.

Charlie cried out, "Yes! The freight elevators

do stop at this floor!" Without waiting for his friend, he ran down the dark halls, shooting his flashlight's beam ahead of him.

After several minutes of searching, however,

he ran his fingers through his rust-colored hair in frustration. "Where are they?"

Brack slowly padded around the corner on his cane. Charlie turned to him. "They're not here," Charlie said. "According to the blueprint, they should be —" He trained his flashlight on a wide panel of sunflower wallpaper. "— right there!"

Brack tilted his head. "I hear something rumbling," he said.

Charlie put his ear to the wall. "The elevator?"

The boy scanned the flowers on the wallpaper. Maybe there was a plaster knob like the two that controlled the ramps to the thirteenth floor.

"Yes, yes!" said Charlie. He found a sunflower whose dark brown head, inside its yellow petals, was sunk at least a quarter of an inch deeper into the wall. A button.

Charlie pressed the button and the flower immediately lit up. "Cool!" he cried. Within a minute a panel, covered in wallpaper, slid soundlessly up and into the ceiling, revealing the freight elevator.

"And look there!" said Charlie. He aimed his flashlight at a far corner of the elevator. The light picked out an orange metal trolley. Thick canvas straps lay at its wheels.

"That would be really useful for moving a statue," said Charlie.

They entered the elevator and Charlie pushed the button for the first floor. With a rumble, the door slid shut. There was no light inside the elevator, so Charlie kept the flashlight on. He did not want to be trapped in the dark again. When the elevator finally jerked to a stop, the back wall opened up, revealing the alley behind the hotel.

The loading docks, thought Charlie.

The storm was gone. Overhead, they could see gray clouds moving in the narrow stretch of sky between old brick buildings. A cool breeze blew into Charlie's face.

A truck delivering bread was backed up to another door alongside them. "This has to be where the crook took the Aphrodite statue," said Charlie. "This is how he got it downstairs. Now we just have to figure out how he got it out of that room, while Tyler was locked inside!"

Shadow Man

Charlie saw a frown of pain flash across Brack's face.

"I think some rest and recuperation is needed," Brack whispered to Charlie.

The boy helped the limping magician back to his house on the roof. Charlie made him lie down on his sofa in the sitting room. Then he waited with his friend while two hours passed across the face of the grandfather clock.

"Hand me that phone," said Brack. "I'm going to see what's holding up that doctor. And you have been wasting far too much time with me." He waved the boy out of the house. "Go! Go investigate!"

Charlie grinned and went looking for Annie at the front desk. Annie smiled when she saw him. "Two words," said Charlie. "Surveillance. Camera."

"You sound just like Tyler," said Annie, leading him into the security room behind. "He's better, by the way. Mrs. Yu called and said he has a slight concussion. And why do you need to see the surveillance camera?"

"I need to see the tapes from today," Charlie said. "By the way, where's Cozette?"

"She said she had a family emergency."

"Oh," said Charlie. "I was going to ask her about those old keys."

"She still has them," said Annie. "At least, I don't see them here at the desk."

She still has them? thought Charlie. *Weird.*

"Which tapes do you need to see?" asked Annie.

"The ones from the loading docks."

"Something happened back there, too?" said Annie.

Charlie explained how he and Brack had discovered that the freight elevator stopped at the thirteenth floor.

It took Annie a while to find the right tapes. Charlie thought he'd go crazy while she typed commands into the computer.

Finally, Annie found the right files and played them back on one of the screens. She asked, "What are you looking for?"

"That!" said Charlie.

The computer screen showed a perfect view of the loading dock next to the freight elevator. A man, dressed all in black, with a black ski mask, was struggling with a heavy object strapped to a trolley, draped in black.

"Who is it?" asked Annie. They both stared closer at the screen.

Charlie frowned. "I can't tell."

They watched the shadowy figure lug the shrouded statue into the back of an SUV. Then the man — they assumed it was a man — closed the loading dock doors, locked the SUV, and walked back into the hotel.

"Now where's he going?" said Annie.

"To get another statue?" said Charlie.

"But that's when we were all upstairs," said Annie. "Look at the time." She pointed to a digital display on the videotape. 12:00. "We got the call from Cozette at 12:30."

"12:30? Are you sure?" said Charlie.

Annie nodded. "I looked at the clock over the front counter when the call came. Then I told a guest who was checking in that I had an emergency and would be right back."

Charlie was confused. "If Ty was attacked right before she called, say 12:29, that means the statue was stolen fifteen minutes before that! But that's impossible! All twelve statues were in the room before Ty pushed us out and locked the door. I saw it!"

At least, I thought I did. I counted twelve statues. Twelve white figures in the darkness.

"I wish we could see who that guy was under all those black clothes," said Annie, staring at the screen again while she replayed the theft. "He was smart to cover up the statue, too," she added. "That way no one could tell what he was moving."

They stared at the frozen image on the screen. The white statue hidden under the black cloth. *That's not a cloth,* Charlie realized. *It's a cape!*

"What's up, you two?" Cozette walked in the room.

"Cozy, I thought you were with your family," said Annie.

Cozette dismissed it with a wave. "Oh, it was a big deal about nothing. It's fine."

"Do you remember what time you called us about Ty?" said Annie.

Cozette pulled out her phone and checked. "It was 12:30. Why?"

"That's what I told Charlie."

Cozette's expression changed. "Um, now that things are a little quieter," she said, "do you think we could go get David Dragonstone's autograph?"

"Oh, Cozette . . ."

"You could take a picture of me next to him," said Cozette. She giggled.

"Oh, that reminds me," said Annie. "I have to send out his white suit to get cleaned before tonight's magic show."

White? thought Charlie. *White and black. Black and white. A black covering over the white statue . . . is that how it was done?*

Twelve statues . . . but not really.

And there was Theopolis standing in the hall, next to Dragonstone, after Ty was attacked. And he would not meet Charlie's gaze. Charlie knew that man would stop at nothing to get the hotel.

Aha! thought Charlie. *Now I know how he did it.*

It was just another magician's trick. And some magicians had assistants.

Ty and the Trap

The twelve priceless statues of Enrico Endriago had been locked in Room 1308 for fifty years. They had been prisoners of the thirteenth floor. And if Charlie was right about who attacked Tyler and why, it all made sense. It explained why, after fifty years, the statues would now be the target of a shadowy figure.

But how could Charlie get the evidence he needed? And how could he tell Annie who he suspected? She'd never believe him.

Annie shook her head at her friend. "Oh, Cozette," she said. "I just don't think it's a good — Tyler!" Annie screamed.

Charlie looked up just as Tyler Yu walked through the door. He wore the same clothes he did when he was carried out on the stretcher four hours earlier. The only thing new about him was a bandage over one eye. Some of his hair was missing at the back of his head. "What are you wimps doing here?" he asked.

"Charlie found the guy who attacked you," said Annie.

The taller boy smacked his hands together. "Yeah? Well, just give me the dude's name. I'll show him. That freak gave me six stitches."

Charlie showed Ty the tape. But Ty was not happy. His spiky hair seemed to grow angrier and spikier. "You can't see who it is!"

"But, uh, I think I might, uh —" said Charlie.

"Hitchcock!" said Ty. "You solved it again?"

"I think so," Charlie said. "But I don't have proof yet."

"Do you have evidence?" asked Cozette. She looked worried.

"Forget proof," said Ty. "Let's go catch this guy!"

"You need evidence," said Cozette. "Otherwise it's just your word against his."

"Or hers," added Annie.

"It's probably a guy," said Cozette. "It usually is."

"Maybe you're right, Ty," said Charlie. "Maybe we do catch him. Or her. But first, we need a trap!"

When Charlie explained his idea, Ty thought it was genius. The two girls were more skeptical, but it was the only way to get the evidence that Brack needed.

Then they started to put the plan into action.

First they printed out a special message on the computer. The message read:

We are happy to announce that Tyler Yu is back and feels much better. He now remembers a valuable clue he left behind in room 1308. He will be sharing that clue with the police tomorrow, and we hope that Ty's attacker will be found and arrested. Then the residents of The Abracadabra can all feel safe once more.

The second step in the trap was to give copies of the message to several people in the hotel. They waited until dinnertime, when they knew people would be busy. Charlie didn't want to meet anyone face to face. Also, preparations for that Saturday night's performance would be in full swing. So they slid the copies under the doors of Dottie Drake, Mr. Madagascar, and Mr. Thursday. A copy was dropped off in the dressing room backstage. They even left one at the front desk so that Rocky would see it. Then Charlie made a few phone calls from the hotel office, spent a few minutes Googling on the computer, and made sure his flashlight batteries were working.

"I think that's everything," said Charlie, when they all met back in the lobby.

"Now's the fun part," said Ty, smacking his fist into his palm.

"Do we have to do this?" asked Cozette, a nervous look on her face.

Annie patted her friend's shoulder. "We'll all be together," she said. "Besides, it will be fun!"

Cozette lifted an eyebrow. "Really? Fun?"

"Thrilling?" suggested Annie.

"How about 'terrifying'?" said Cozette.

Charlie agreed. He wasn't looking forward to this part of the plan. And less than twenty minutes later, as he stood in Room 1308 in pitch darkness, he had to force down panic. It bubbled

up inside his chest and into his throat. *I am not going to scream*, he told himself.

Charlie was standing behind the statue of Hades, lord of the dead. The other three kids were hidden behind various statues.

Charlie felt dizzy. He leaned against the statue.

"I hear something," whispered Annie.

They all froze. "I think that's my heart pounding," said Cozette. "I have something I need to confess."

Charlie's mind rapidly pieced new clues together. Had he been wrong all this time? Was the criminal Cozette? She carried keys to the old rooms of the thirteenth floor. She had recently started working at the hotel, right before Brack disappeared. When she came out of Room 1308 when Tyler was hurt, she could easily had locked the room behind her. After she had knocked him out!

And when Charlie tried to unlock it, and the

key wouldn't work, there was only one expla-
nation. She had given him the wrong key on
purpose.

Cozette could have moved that statue by
herself, too. She could have used the trolley. And
when the thief was caught on videotape, where
was she?

But why would she do it?

Charlie heard Cozette gasp. A flashlight
beam, from outside the room, was traveling
along the bottom edge of the door. Someone was
standing just outside.

Someone gripped the doorknob. Charlie
heard a scrape, then a rustle. The lock was being
fiddled with. Then — *click*!

Charlie took a deep breath. He felt the hairs
on the back of his neck prickling up like ant
feelers.

"Lights!" Charlie shouted. The four of them
switched on their flashlights as one, aiming at
the intruder.

The figure lifted its arms. It tried to hide, but they could see exactly who it was.

Ancestors

"David Dragonstone!"

The young magician lowered his arms and squinted into their flashlights. "What — what's going on?"

Tyler stepped out from behind a statue that held twin thunderbolts.

Charlie thought his friend looked angry

enough to start throwing thunderbolts of his own.

"You're the jerk who hit me!" Ty said.

"It was an accident," cried Dragonstone. "An accident!"

"It was no accident when you stole that statue of Aphrodite," said Annie.

"You kids are nuts," said Dragonstone. He quickly turned to exit the room, but the door was locked. He rattled the knob, but it still wouldn't open.

"How do you like our magic trick, Dragonstone?" said Ty.

Dragonstone turned to face them. His eyes gleamed angrily. "What are you doing in here, anyway?" he demanded.

"What are you doing here?" asked Annie.

"He's looking for that clue I supposedly remembered that would point to his guilt," said Ty. "But there is no clue, Dragonstone. We just made that up."

"It's a trap," said Charlie.

A feeling of relief hit him like sunshine through an open door. He was glad his first hunch was right. Cozette was innocent. But then, what had she been close to confessing before Dragonstone arrived?

Dragonstone laughed. "A trap? Don't be stupid. I just came in here to take a look at these incredible sculptures."

"But you've seen them before," said Charlie. "Plenty of times. Probably in old photographs that belonged to your grandfather. Or was it your uncle?"

Dragonstone was silent.

"I looked him up on the computer," said Charlie. "Ernesto Endriago. Endriago means 'dragon' in Spanish. And that's where you're from. Spain."

"Anyone could have known about these statues," said the magician.

"Only Brack and Ernesto knew about them,"

said Charlie. "They got delivered to the wrong floor and ended up locked in this room for years. Only those two men knew about them. Or whoever they told. And I thought it was weird that in all this time, after fifty years, that now is when someone tried to steal them. The first time you ever performed at the Abracadabra."

"Pure coincidence," said Dragonstone, folding his arms. "I have nothing to do with this."

"You just said it was an accident that you hit Tyler!" Annie pointed out.

"Did I?" said Dragonstone. "I must have been shocked by the flashlights. I didn't know what I was saying. Besides," he added, leaning against the wall, "it's my word against yours. You have no proof."

"Think again. We got plenty of proof, you creep," said Ty.

Charlie noticed a bead of sweat forming on Dragonstone's pale forehead. "We have a videotape," Charlie said. "It shows a man carrying a statue into an SUV."

"Does it?" said Dragonstone. "Does it show a man, or does it show me? Can you see my face?"

"You know we can't," said Charlie. "Because you were wearing a mask. But we did see something. We saw the SUV. And we saw the license plate. And we can give that number to the police and find out who owns it."

Suddenly, the door swung open. "We already have," said Brack. Behind him stood three police officers.

The men crowded into the room. The police also carried flashlights, and Dragonstone was snared in the web of their beams. "We also found a pair of keys belonging to the SUV in your room, Mr. Dragonstone," said one of the officers. "And right now we're examining the SUV. We found it parked a few blocks away from the hotel."

"This is ridiculous," said Dragonstone. "First of all, how could I possibly have been in this room, when your friend here got injured, when I was outside all the time?"

Charlie smiled. "Because you weren't outside. You were inside all the time!"

Then he explained how the magician had managed his trick.

Dragonstone had stolen the statue of Aphrodite, loading it off the dock and into his SUV. That was around 12:15.

Then he returned to the hotel. He planned to steal a second statue. Dragonstone was inside Room 1308 when Charlie, Ty, and Cozette entered.

It was too late to find a hiding place, so Dragonstone stood off in a corner, frozen. In the dim light of a flashlight, and wearing his trademark white suit, he blended in with the statues. Charlie had seen him out of the corner of his eyes, but had mistaken him for a statue. That's why Charlie had thought all twelve of them were in the room.

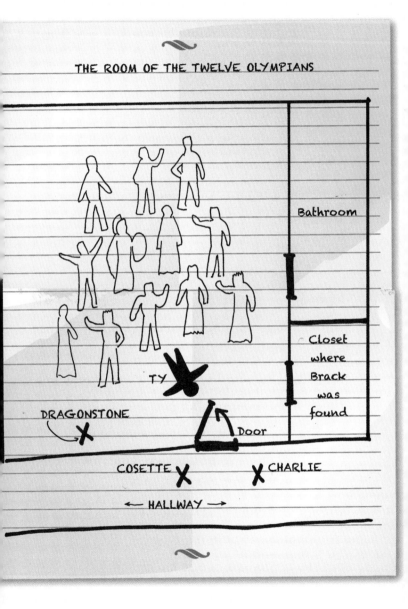

THE ROOM OF THE TWELVE OLYMPIANS

Bathroom

Closet where Brack was found

TY

DRAGONSTONE

Door

COSETTE

CHARLIE

← HALLWAY →

Then, after Ty pushed Cozette and Charlie into the hall and locked the door, Dragonstone tried to find a better hiding place. But he was afraid Ty might see him. So he knocked him out.

"I would never be so brutal," cried Dragonstone.

"That's where you're wrong," came a voice from the doorway.

"Theopolis!" cried Charlie.

The evil magician, wearing his dark cape, looked angry and sad at the same time. He starred at his young partner. "You and I had coffee with Brack in his home the other night," he said. "I was in disguise, because I know how Brack feels about me."

Brack was silent.

"And then when he unmasked me," continued Theopolis, "I left and returned to my room. But you stayed behind." He pointed to Dragonstone. "I found out that Brack had vanished the next day. I decided to use it to my advantage and finally take over this hotel. But I did not realize who had kidnapped Brack, until I saw this room today. Then I knew. You are the grandson of the famous Ernesto Endriago, and I knew he had sent the statues here. Brack had told me about them, many years ago. But I had forgotten all about them. Until today."

Theopolis turned to Brack. "I am sorry about all this," he said in a low voice. "I had no idea to what depths Ernesto's grandson would sink!"

"That still doesn't explain how we saw Mr. Dragonstone come in from the hall after Tyler was attacked," said Cozette. "How could he get out of the room?"

"He never did!" said Charlie. "After hitting Ty, he hid beside the door, in the dark. He used the black cape that he covered up the statues with, to hide himself. To melt into the shadows, unseen. Then when Rocky broke down the door, everyone started crowding into the room. Dragonstone just joined the crowd. No one noticed how he got there. We were all too busy looking at Ty."

"Look!" shouted Annie. She aimed her flashlight at a dark corner of the room near the door. "There's the cape! It's proof!"

Then the room burst into chaos. Dragonstone waved his hand and an explosion lit up the room like a firework. People shouted and screamed and ran toward the door. And after all the pushing and shoving and jostling, a police officer cried, "Dragonstone! He's gone!"

The officers split up and ran down several hallways, searching for the magician.

"It was flashpowder," said Theopolis grimly. "An old trick."

"The old tricks are the best tricks," said Brack.

Annie turned to her friend. "Cozy," she said. "Remember earlier, when you said you had something to confess?"

Cozette blushed. "I couldn't take being in

the room any longer. I had to tell you guys that I'm afraid of the dark!"

"Just like brainiac here," said Tyler, nodding toward Charlie.

Theopolis cleared his throat loudly and then said, "I shall go and tell our audience there's been a change of plans."

"Wait!" said Brack, holding up a hand. "A change, yes. But not a cancellation."

Theopolis stared at his former partner and frowned. "You mean —?"

"We'll go on instead," said Brack. "You and I. I'm sure we can improvise a show. A good show, too."

"But what about Dragonstone?" asked Charlie.

"Oh, I doubt if the police will find him this time," said Brack. "He's far too clever. But at least you and your friends foiled his plans. And saved the hotel from losing millions of dollars worth of art!"

"What do we do now?" asked Tyler.

Brack bowed to him over his cane. "You run downstairs and grab the best seat in the house, young man. For the show must go on!"

MICHAEL DAHL grew up reading everything he could find about his hero Harry Houdini, and worked as a magician's assistant when he was a teenager. Even though he cannot disappear, he is very good at escaping things. Dahl has written the popular Library of Doom series, the Dragonblood books, and the Finnegan Zwake series. He currently lives in the Midwest in a haunted house.

LISA K. WEBER is an illustrator currently living in Oakland, California. She graduated from Parsons School of Design in 2000 and then began freelancing. Since then, she has completed many print, animation, and design projects, including graphic novelizations of classic literature, character and background designs for children's cartoons, and textiles for dog clothing.